✓ **P9-BBT-627**

9/16/0d

The Lives of Shadows

The Lives of Shadows

Barbara Hodgson

CHRONICLE BOOKS
SAN FRANCISCO

All uncredited archival images are from Byzantium Archives. Every
effort has been made to trace accurate ownership of copyrighted text
and visual material used in this book. Errors or omissions will be
corrected in subsequent editions, provided notification is sent to the
publisher. Page 186 constitutes a continuation of the copyright page.

LIBRARY OF CONGRESS CATALOGING-IN-PUBLICATION DATA:

Hodgson, Barbara, 1955–
        The lives of shadows / Barbara Hodgson.
            p. cm.
        ISBN 0-8118-3926-5
    1. British—Syria—Fiction. 2. Damascus (Syria)—Fiction. 3. Home
ownership—Fiction. 4. Haunted houses—Fiction. I. Title.
        PS3558.O34345L58 2004
        813'.54—DC21   2003007904

Manufactured in China

Design by Barbara Hodgson/Byzantium Books

Distributed in Canada by Raincoast Books
9050 Shaughnessy Street
Vancouver, BC V6P 6E5

10 9 8 7 6 5 4 3 2 1

Chronicle Books LLC
85 Second Street
San Francisco, CA 94105

www.chroniclebooks.com

TO DAVID

Julian

mark + ?

AFTERNOON

JULIAN SHOULD HAVE NEVER ANSWERED THE DOOR. The knocking was too insistent, too loud. It sounded like trouble. But, like a fool, he let his curiosity get the better of him; he unlocked the door and let the trouble in.

A short, stout man, wearing an exquisitely tailored three-piece suit, pushed his way past as though he thought he owned the place. Which, as it turned out, he did.

He was followed by a younger, somewhat shabby and insignificant fellow, who clutched a sheaf of papers. Each jauntily balanced a tarboosh—the headgear of choice for professional men—on his head. A squarely built, uniformed official bringing up the rear sported a beret known locally as a *sidara*. It gave him the swagger of a bodyguard.

Without a word of explanation, the three strangers spilled into the courtyard, poisoning the tranquil air with their presence. Julian would not have been surprised to see the roses and jasmine wilt as they neared. They strolled around the fountain, inspected the marble, dipped their fingers in the water, frowned at the fallen leaves. Their boldness cautioned Julian to hold his tongue and wait for them to justify their intrusion. He asked himself all the while if he knew them from somewhere, but he could dredge up no recollection whatsoever.

When the official pointed to the delicate plasterwork over one of the doors, prompting nods and sighs from the other two, Julian speculated they were scouting for movie locales; he'd heard that another house had recently been used in an Egyptian film. That would explain the rudeness. But he decided they were tax collectors when the younger man with the papers spun around, his previously placid expression now hard. After shuffling his papers, the man raised them ceremoniously, cleared his throat, and began to read aloud.

French and Arabic legalese poured out, merging into an incomprehensible stream. Julian understood the individual words—*bait, parcelle, titre de propriété, référence cadastrale, as-sijill*, all had to do with property—though he struggled to make sense of how they were put together and what they had to do with him. The speaker glared when he finished, as if defending himself against protest or rebuttal, but Julian was incapable of any response whatsoever.

Then the words rearranged themselves with disturbing clarity, and he suddenly understood that the middle-aged man was the husband of a niece of Nasim Katib, the man from whom he had bought the house, and that the younger man was his lawyer. Their visit had nothing to do with movies or taxes or anything else Julian might have imagined. They'd come for his home, Bait Katib, one of the oldest houses in Damascus.

Evening

Looking back on the day, Julian wondered why he hadn't expected this visit. Several years earlier a lawyer had written, warning that relatives of the long-deceased Nasim Katib were planning to contest his title to Bait Katib. He had exchanged letters with the lawyer, challenging the proposed action, but their correspondence had died out—possibly due to the family's lack of funds—and he forgot the matter entirely. Now it appeared they had scraped together the means to carry on. How they had kept him out of the process was a mystery.

His calmness in light of the shock he had received surprised him. Even though Bait Katib ran like blood through his veins, his first instinct had been to let it go; his revulsion of combat was that strong. Now that he was alone with the wretched document, however, he snapped out of his complacence. He'd protest, he'd appeal, he would relinquish nothing without a fight.

He sat down at his desk in the study that was unchanged since his first day in the house and spread out the document. Then he laid his head upon it, his jaw, cheek, temple, ear, pressing into the sharp, antagonizing words. Why punish himself further by rereading these words? He'd already been dragged through every sentence by the men, who had refused to leave until he'd signed each page in acknowledgment of the contents. This had been laboriously achieved over many cigarettes and glasses of tea, followed by tumblers of potent, milky *'araq,* for though he despised their mission, he was not a bad host.

Without raising his head, he pictured the words stacked in two columns, mirroring each other: French on the left and Arabic on the right. The first page summarized the claim and listed his name, Julian Beaufort, and his address, Bait Katib, Harat al-Hariqa,

Damascus, Syria. He always marveled that such a simple address sufficed in a city of more than a quarter million people.

Farther down was the date when his deed was signed, September 17th, 1914, and the date when it was found to be invalid, May 18th, 1945. Below was the date by which he was supposed to leave—May 30th, 1945—in just six short days. Then came details about the self-proclaimed new titleholder and a mass of signatures, stamps, and seals. The document's dozen or so pages described the building's condition and size, its features and furnishings, plan and site numbers, and estimated worth. On page nine was a proposal to pay compensation for improvements made over the years. On page ten that exact sum was charged back for outstanding rent and costs. Appended were affidavits from notaries, bankers, and other interested parties.

Still with his head on the desk, he squinted at the papers stretched out before him, hoping, through the distorted perspective, to transform them into a field of harmless scribbles. Instead, the sight was a reminder of what wasn't written down. His future, for example. What was to happen to him if they were successful? Bait Katib was everything to him, everything he had worked for, his only home, his refuge.

Slowly, tears began streaming down his face. They rolled onto the document, and when, in sudden fury, he crushed it in his hands, the ink smeared. He pushed it aside, letting it fall onto the floor, and wiped his face on his shirtsleeve. It's the shock; pull yourself together, he scolded himself. Get organized and fight this.

What to do first? Visions of judges, land titles offices, and lawyers jammed his brain and spun his thoughts round. He shook them away. What he needed was proof of ownership. All at once, he leaped for the door, the desk drawers, the shelves. Just as suddenly, he paused. What if these proofs, these deeds, letters, and receipts that he'd amassed over the years, were dismissed as trivial detritus from the past? In that case, maybe he could argue the right of current possession. It was the strongest single proof of ownership in this country, had been for centuries, but would it apply to him, still a foreigner in spite of his twenty years of living there?

It was no good, his thoughts flying helter-skelter like this. He needed to catch them and write them down. The thing would be to chronicle his occupation of the house, from the day he moved in, right up to the present. He switched on the desk lamp and removed a notebook from the drawer. Opening to the first page, he wrote "November 2nd, 1925."

Now what? Should he explain how he had come to own the house, or should he skip to when he moved in? He went and took down a half-dozen books from shelves inset into the far wall. From an adjacent wooden chest, he drew out rolls of paper. Over the course of the next half hour, he made many trips back and forth between the shelves, chest, and desk, trampling the document underfoot with relish, thinking all the while about the best approach.

Searching for the right books, the necessary papers, took his mind off that afternoon's unpleasant meeting. He even began looking forward to the task ahead. The idea of plotting a strategy gave him the sensation that he had nothing to fear. He lapsed into absentminded humming, at one point breaking off and saying aloud, "You like that song, don't you?" Looking round the study, he then smiled, saying, "I could use your help, you know. Ah, it's no use, I mustn't go crazy. Then they really would take the house away." He continued humming, the smile now gone from his lips but still visible through his sparkling, purposeful eyes.

When the desk's surface became too crowded to accommodate the growing mass of material, he laid the overflow on the floor, covering up the hateful document. Then, engulfed with photographs, sketches, maps, ink, pens, pencils, glue, and brushes, he started his account.

November 2nd, 1925, Beirut to Damascus

The house was bringing me back to Damascus. And now I was almost really there, after eleven years of anticipation, of planning and longing and of declaring, every single year of those eleven interminable years, that next year I would return, next year I would live in my house.

I can remember looking at my watch and timing my arrival. Eight minutes till the train pulled into Beramke station, a few minutes to get my bearings and find a taxi, a ten-minute ride if the traffic was heavy, and a five-minute walk down narrow alleys. If I could have sped up the train I would have, yet in some absurd way I also wanted to stretch out my arrival. I must have been reluctant to surrender the sensation of longing that I had lived with for so long.

I don't remember exactly, but I'm sure I reached into my pocket and felt for the deed for the thousandth, no, ten thousandth time. I knew it by heart: *Bait Katib of al-Bab al-Jabiyya quarter is hereby transferred from Nasim Katib to Julian Beaufort, on this day, the 17th of September, 1914.* Signed two days before I left to go back to a Europe by then irrevocably engaged in war.

I'd stumbled across the house during my graduation trip through Egypt and Syria, which I suppose could have been called a watered-down, 1914 version of the Grand Tour. While on this trip I'd discovered—to my shame—that outwardly I was the same as all the other young travelers I encountered. Whether they were eighteen, or twenty-five, or twenty-two, as I was, each one had the impression that these exotic lands existed for him alone. We all waxed romantic about the soft, languid nights; the furtively seductive looks bestowed upon us by veiled women; and the intoxication of smoking a narghile in dark and mysterious cafés, where our overworked imaginations saw great plots being hatched by ruthless men slyly fingering the tips of savage mustaches, the likes of which we aspired to in vain.

But by the time I'd sailed in a felucca to Aswan, trekked by camel across the Sinai to Petra, and ridden with a caravan into Damascus, I knew that my love for the East was different from the others', even though I followed their well-trodden path. I belonged to this part of the world. I felt it with every nerve, every instinct. Any attempt to live elsewhere would have been a sham. It wasn't an esoteric yearning but, rather, an emotion that hits you when the rhythm and temperament in a certain place matches your own to a degree that you've never experienced before. Within the enduring, sepia-toned walls of Damascus especially, I envisioned a place for myself with such clarity that leaving threatened to break my heart. I vowed to thwart fate.

My original plan had been to make my way from Damascus to Constantinople and back to London, where an engineering position in a city firm awaited. The job was a real plum that I'd been pleased to land but, after months of travel, the thought of working steady hours—never one of my strengths—had become unbearable. It wasn't just the idea of routine that got to me. I knew I wouldn't fit in an established hierarchy, and I'd either be sacked for insubordination or submerge my spirit so thoroughly that I'd destroy myself.

Going home meant facing a future where every miserable step was preordained: a job at the same desk until age sixty-five, a bed-sit choked with the fumes of coal fires half the year, then maybe marriage to a pinched-face stranger with a couple of kiddies tossed in as further aggravation. Surrounded by busybodies who have your caste and income pegged with malicious accuracy. Where history is something you wallpaper over, intelligence something you reveal only to a select few, true happiness a luxury.

Then there was the growing possibility of war. In the face of this, my lackluster enthusiasm for returning faded into nonexistence.

Every day I found another excuse to stay, and each of those days flew by as quickly as a stolen hour. Perhaps I thought that no one would be able to take back the purloined time if I smuggled it into the labyrinthine streets of the old city. At any rate, that's where I often found myself, and with each exploration of the twisting, narrow lanes, I seemed to be unwinding a length of thread behind me. Instead of guiding me back to the exit, however, the thread tangled itself around me, holding me resolutely.

I might have tried to break that thread, if it weren't for the houses. Disguised outwardly as humble wattle-and-daub tenements, they revealed their sumptuous interiors reluctantly. A long passageway or a half-open door might hint of a sun-drenched garden, a private courtyard, colorful tile work, but nothing more. Frustrated and enchanted, I began brazenly knocking at all doors and thus invited myself into many houses. In every instance, I was welcomed unquestioningly, as if the residents were fully aware of my unqualified admiration for their homes. They showed me what it would be like to live in a place that was an integral part of oneself, a place that looked inward, reflecting one's past and future, but only to those chosen to see.

So many travelers are beguiled by the idea of living in foreign lands, but when the time comes to return home, they do so without lasting regret. For my part, I couldn't imagine quelling such a deep longing. If I'd been married, I'd have left my wife; if I'd been the sole support of aged parents, I'd have cut them adrift; if I'd been on the ladder to fame and fortune, I would have gladly slid back down to the bottom. At the same time, I had no illusions about the difficulties of turning my desire into reality. Used to being buffeted about by circum-stance, I now took my future into my own hands and sought for ways and means to stay. This meant applying for jobs at schools, the consulate, import/export companies. To no avail. I wired my guardian and entreated him to release my funds, which were in trust until I turned twenty-five. That his response was a cutting "no" didn't surprise me. Concrete methods failing, I daydreamed of inheritances from remote relatives, hoping that a strong enough wish would make it so. At the very least, these occupations delayed my departure.

One day early in August, fate brought me to a house near Bab al-Jabiyya, the Gate of the Well, in the western section of the old city. My knock was answered by an elderly but still-spry gentleman to whom I explained the purpose of my visit. Nasim Katib ushered me in and offered coffee, as was the custom. We talked about his house and his work—he was a scribe and calligrapher—and I was immediately struck by his profound knowledge of Damascus architecture and history. I left with an invitation to return for dinner the following evening. That was when I met his wife, Muna, and his daughter, Asilah.

The consequent move out of the hotel and into the room that's directly above this study seemed natural and inevitable. For the following month, as a guest of the Katibs, I spent much of my time at the house doing nothing in particular. In the mornings, I joined Nasim's small group of students and listened to the murmur of their voices and the scratching of their reed pens. In the afternoons, I drank tea and chatted or sketched or read. Evenings lasted well into the night with late dinners made up of endless streams of *mazza*, or tidbits, often followed by Muna playing the oud and, if she was there, Asilah singing with a captivating voice that haunted me long after the music ended. Nasim and Muna saw straight off that the music went right to my head. They'd tease me with the titles of the songs: "May the Judge of Love Dispense Justice to You," or "The Moon Is Pale before Your Face," and threaten to marry me off to a Damascus girl. Maybe because she herself was soon to be married, Asilah never took part in the banter.

Despite its modest size, the house stood out in my mind as especially fine, distinguished from the others by the courtyard that had been transformed by Nasim into a kind of vertical book. Every surface of wall not already covered with tile or carved wood was written upon in relief, the words incised into plaster. This was Nasim's history of his family. The work had taken him decades and wasn't yet complete.

I had never realized that an inanimate building could be

brought to life in such a way and crazily conceived the notion that I could somehow become part of that history. Nasim was so natural and guileless that before I knew it, I had confided this to him. Soon after, he asked me if I'd like to buy his house. I could

Tekiyye al-Sulaimaniyya   *Faculté de droit*

Qanawat

have shouted with joy. My innate pragmatism immediately and thoroughly withered. I didn't dare ask why he was proposing to sell it to me, lest he come to his senses and withdraw the offer. And I didn't even think of whether or not I could afford such a thing, how I would get the money, or if, as a foreigner, I would be permitted to own property.

By mid-September, the details were worked out with the help of George Samad, a notary whose enviable sleight-of-hand manipulations managed the negotiations, sped up the transfer of documents and deed translations, ensured that I understood the complicated language, and arranged for witnesses. I paid a token deposit with the promise to send the rest from London on my return there, along with a definite date for moving in.

As for the Katibs, Asilah was to move in with her in-laws, but I urged Nasim and Muna to remain. I would never ask them to leave. They were too much a part of the house, and I had come to think of them as family. As it turned out, Nasim died very shortly after. I suspect he sold me the house because he wanted Muna to have money to live on and not to be burdened with a costly, overlarge house like Bait Katib. And he trusted Asilah, or me, to make sure she had a roof over her head.

So, I was going to ignore the war, clear up my few obligations, return to Damascus, and somehow make a living. To a twenty-two-year-old, nothing could have been more feasible. But back in England, I realized it wasn't going to be so easy. I wasn't as flush as I thought, travel having drained my bank account, and my guardian—an uncle on my father's side, still puffed up from his triumphs against the Boers—pressured me to follow his lead and join the Royal Engineers. He only succeeded by stooping to blackmail, promising the money I needed if I enlisted. Vexed but over a barrel, I caved in, wired the balance due on the house, and wrote that my return would be delayed for a few months.

Then the war fouled up all my plans.

These years are difficult for me to write about, though I suppose I must try to explain what kept me away from Bait Katib. For a start, the war lasted far longer than anyone ever dared imagine. Short of getting carried out feet first or deserting and ending up as target practice for a firing squad, once you were in, there was no way out. I had deluded myself into believing that as a civil engineer I'd have it easy, building or destroying bridges, camps, roads, railways, and trenches. It was fun and games for the first few months. We were constantly on our toes and, even though highly regimented, enjoyed a great deal of independence. What I hadn't counted on was that we were always the first at the front.

I had made a copy of the deed to take with me, and while other men cherished letters from their sweethearts, I had my deed and my dreams of the house. With all the rain and mud and sweat at the front, paper stood an even smaller chance of survival than I did, so I ended up copying it out at least a dozen times before my discharge in 1917. That sacred piece of paper was always within grasp. If my fingers were too cold and numb to feel it, I'd spin into a panic that took ages to calm. Life then was so irrational that, if I hadn't had the deed to turn to, I would have lost my mind.

And I almost did lose it, in another sense. By 1917 I could congratulate myself on having stayed in one piece for three years. That was three years of wallowing in cold, septic mud, next to fellows rotting, getting blown up, or both. I envied the ones who got it over with fast. Words can't describe the horror of crawling among men with no legs or no face who refuse to die.

Then it was my turn. I was on the Arras road to see about supplies when a high-pitched whine tore past and a mess of shells burst in front of me. I jumped from the wagon and hit the ground, scrabbling to dig myself in. The shelling stopped. I waited a few minutes before getting up to continue on my way. Then the Germans threw everything they had at me, and a cold wind ricocheted through my head. Suddenly, I was the chap refusing to die.

I came out of a coma six months later, chunks of shrapnel still lodged in my brain, and my first words, so the nurse told me, were "Where is it? Where's my house?" A while later she brought me the two things they'd found on me: the tattered, bloodstained copy of the deed and a key. They were all I needed to get started mending.

The surgeon left much of the shrapnel where it was, fearing the consequences of removing it. After a year, I was released from hospital but had a relapse that put me back in for another six months. The injury affected my limbs somehow, and out of the blue my legs would forget to work. I was advised not to travel, but I got ready to depart anyway. Having come so close to death, I only feared being buried alive in London. My trust freed up during the war, giving me my independence, then my uncle died and left me some more money, along with a complicated estate to clear up. Whenever I thought I'd finished with England, another chore kept me there. I booked my passage a

Kafer Sur

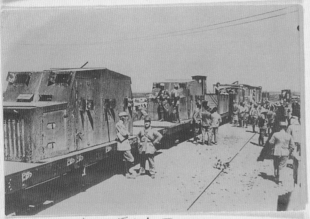

Viscontin: Jebel Druze

dozen times yet never lost my faith that one of those times would be for keeps.

I haven't explained the key. It was another talisman, a cumbersome thing of true Ottoman proportions. Nasim had threaded it onto a leather strap and, with much solemnity, hung it around my neck, saying, "From now on, only you will be able to open this door." I never took it off. It lay heavily against my chest—shedding rusty chips and powder trails onto my skin—a constant reminder of why I had to pull through, especially when there were precious few reasons to carry on. After the war it became a kind of personal recrimination for not being strong enough to recover and then, once I was back on my feet, for not being courageous enough to cut my ties and return to Damascus. It was around my neck, still, on this November morning. Eleven years late, its magic was finally working.

And now I was so close. My heart was pounding. I looked out the train window to calm myself. There was Jebel Kasyoun, the hill to the north, and there the viaduct, running parallel to the tracks. The brakes whined, and passengers who had already risen were thrown off balance by the abrupt change in speed. The old gent who had been my neighbor for the trip from Beirut

16

fell onto my lap, so I helped him back up and made a show of brushing him off. We laughed at each other; then, still smiling at me, he spoke to a rather dour fellow who was also in the compartment. This man sucked his teeth and said something under his breath. The old man, now scowling, mimicked shooting a rifle. For a second, when he pointed the imaginary weapon at me, I actually felt sick to my stomach. Then he asked, "*Soldat?*" I shook my head. The two men turned around abruptly and left the compartment.

There was no need to wonder what that had been about. Soldiers were in abundance here, brought by the French to suppress uprisings, especially in the Jebel Druze, the mountainous region south of Damascus. And they were not loved. In retrospect, I don't think there was a correct way of responding to the old man's question. If I wasn't a soldier, what the hell was I doing here, and if I was, then why didn't I get the hell out?

Because the unrest had been in the international papers since August, all eyes were on Syria. But for me, so preoccupied with finally being able to return, this news had scarcely registered, until I reached Beirut ten days earlier, that is. There I learned that, in retaliation for the barbaric public hanging of more than twenty Druze corpses in Damascus, rebels had slain and mutilated a dozen Circassian irregulars and had insolently dumped them at the gate to the Christian quarter. Rioting had followed, to which the French replied with shelling and aerial bombardment. Brutal behavior on both sides led to the devastation of the section of the old city within which stood my house. I told myself that the situation couldn't possibly be so gruesome, for if it were true, then Bait Katib might no longer exist. Lecturing myself was futile; every second spent not knowing the fate of my house was agony, like a fever.

Beirut had been overrun with military, and the sole purpose of every soldier there was to get in my way. Walking up a street

L'Illustration
14 Nov. 1925

DAMAS BRÛLE

BEYROUTH, le 27 octobre :

De tous les côtés de la ville les hordes se précipitèrent vers le palais Azem, mais il était solidement défendu. La porte monumentale ne cédait pas, les mitrailleuses fauchaient, il n'y avait aucun moyen d'y pénétrer autrement que par un incendie qui abattrait ses murs. Et de monstrueuses flammes de s'élever dans le ciel, dévorant la résidence et le superbe salon, d'une si grande valeur, principal pavillon de ce vaste et unique édifice de l'art arabe. Les murs s'écroulèrent et, de par les brèches, les vandales s'introduisirent dans le palais, qui fut littéralement saccagé. On a tout emporté. Les archives traînaient encore par terre et dans la cour. Elles avaient été complètement bouleversées, ce qui démontre que tout a été fouillé et pillé. Seul le coffrefort est resté inviolable et, lorsque les tanks eurent délogé les insurgés de là, il fut mis en sûreté ailleurs. Mais que pouvait-il contenir ?... Toutes les richesses étaient étalées dans les salles et les vitrines, aujourd'hui brisées, vides. D'après M. Doummar, secrétaire du service de l'Institut, les débris s'élèvent à quatre millions de

Souk el-Hamidiyeh

LES ÉVÉNEMENTS DE SYRIE

◆

Le ministère des Affaires étrangères a communiqué, le 1 novembre, un rapport officiel qu'il avait enfin reçu sur les troubles de Damas. Ce document tend à réduire à de moindres proportions l'étendue de l'émeute et les conséquences du bombardement. Les pertes françaises y sont indiquées comme étant d'une dizaine de morts et d'une centaine de blessés ; celles des rebelles, de 300 tués. En outre, une cinquantaine d'Arméniens auraient été massacrés. En ce qui concerne les dégâts, ils seraient limités aux quartiers indigènes dans lesquels, est-il précisé « aucune construction arabe présentant

---

REVOLT DAMASC

LA TURQUIE 1925

CITY SHELLED BY THE FRENCH.

REBELS DEFEATED.

(FROM OUR CORRESPONDENT.)
HAIFA, Oct. 20.

Until Monday afternoon a large part of Damascus was in the hands of insurgents and rioters, while the French garrison, to the number of some 2,000 men, who held the principal building in the centre and completely dominated the town from the heights of Salihiyeh, bombarded them. All communication by road was temporarily interrupted and the insurgents damaged the railway between Meidan and Beramkeh.

BEIRUT, Oct. 20.

According to the latest information from Damascus, Druse insurgents who had secretly entered the southern suburbs of Damascus were joined by a number of rioters who barricaded the Moslem

quarters and burned some shops houses. Fire was opened on who held the public building ry from Salihiyeh quarters all o ured cars playe s a rioters. T

---

e Institut d'Art et han. Its director is M. ontained many rare objects, including all recent archaeological discoveries in Syria, and was renowned for its marble fittings and mosaic work. Practically none of these treasures remain. Brigands either looted or deliberately smashed them—pieces on the ground reveal what the Vandal hands did—while shell fire has barely left the walls standing of the handsome haramlik. The brigands also paid attention to the palace which General Sarrail recently selected as a pied-à-terre during his periodical visits to Damascus. The General had left it only that morning for Deraa, and by evening his apartments had been reduced to ruins by shells which rained on the palace as soon as it was known that the brigands had seized it.

The sweetmeat bazaar "El Bzourieh" near by is seriously damaged, and a shop, the famous "Dalale," is completely destroyed.

The houses of such well-known families as Ali Riza Pasha er Rikabit, the Emir Abdullah's Premier, and the Bakris, who joined Sultan Atrash, and the Kawatly, all have been completely destroyed. The house of Kawatly was one of the show places and was, like the Azm Palace, a gem of Arabesque art. These are but some of the buildings of the damaged area. Words fail describe

movemen a radius of 1 all movemen the area wit

Railway Time-Table

STATIONS.	Time of Arrival.	Time of Departure.	STATIONS.	Time of Arrival.	Time of Departure.
	A.M.	A.M.		P.M.	P.M.
Beyrout-Port . .	—	7.0	Rayak	—	12.45
Beyrout Station .	7.13	7.17	Yahfoufah . . .	1.10	1.15
Hadett	7.35	7.38	Zerghaya	1.41	1.42
Babda	7.54	7.55	Zebdâni	2.4	2.9
Jamhour . . .	8.13	8.18	Et Tequieh . . .	2.34	2.35
Araya	8.40	8.45	Souk-Barada . .	2.44	2.46
Aley	9.11	9.17	Deir-Ilhanoûn . .	2.54	2.55
Béhamdoûn . .	9.47	9.50	Aïn Figéh . . .	3.5	3.9
Sofar	10.12	10.17	Jédeideh . . .	3.23	3.24
Beidar	10.43	10.44	Haméh	3.32	3.36
Méréjat . . .	11.2	11.6	Doummar . . .	3.44	3.45
Jéditha-Chtaura .	11.18	11.20	Damascus-Béramké	4.0	4.12
Saïd-Neil . . .	11.32	11.33	Damascus-Midân	4.25	—
Mouallaka . .	11.43	11.55			
Rayak (Buffet) .	12.15	P.M.			

was like swimming against an unrelenting current, and getting a room for oneself was next to impossible. A somber carnival atmosphere had settled in, polluted with ugly, drunken soldiers and even uglier tarts, and tinged with suspicion and hostility, contrasting grimly with the gay hospitality of a decade previous. Chaos ruled, and in the confusion, I had a hell of a time getting accurate information about travel. When I tried to find a ride to Damascus, I was told that the road was blocked and that fighting was intense. As for trains, I was told that a segment of the track between the two cities had been blown up; a lie, as it turned out, though attempts had been made to obstruct it.

Trains were running, but could I buy a ticket? The clerk laughed in my face, so I begged an American reporter at my hotel to get one for me. By this point I was ready to walk, I was that desperate. At last, with my ticket in hand, I left my steamer trunk—the sum total of my worldly belongings, aside from the small valise I kept with me—to be called for, if fate was on my side. By the time I boarded the train, I was a wreck.

We finally pulled into Damascus's Beramke station. A scrum of panicked travelers fought to get on the train as we fought to get off. I'd never seen such a madhouse. Boxes were flung up onto our feet and into our legs, tripping us up as we tried to descend. A woman got knocked out by a flying sack. Another clung to my sleeve but was swept away all the same. The din was incredible. Once I escaped the platform, however, I could see that the station, a small, squat building, looked the same as when I'd left eleven years before, except that now it overflowed with what seemed to be a League of Nations's selection of soldiery:

North African spahis, sporting turbans; Senegalese and Malagasy *tirailleurs*, decked out in fezzes; and French officers, in kepis. Some rigid with attention, some smoking lazily, some crouched on the floor or flopped against duffel bags, all with rifles slung over their shoulders or braced against their chests.

Life was evidently carrying on, despite the rebellion. Vendors threaded their way through the crowds, selling nuts, cigarettes, or water. Begging children yanked on robes and coats. Porters relieved new arrivals of their bags and steered them through the doors.

An especially feeble old porter attached himself to me, perhaps having assessed my ability to carry my small bag myself. He halfheartedly wrestled with it but gave up easily when I wouldn't let go. All the same, he looked as though he needed work, so I figured I'd have him get me a cab. First I tried telling him the address, but my accent obviously mangled the words. Then I printed out the address, my nerves having obliterated my little stockpile of Arabic script. He looked at the note, nodded with what turned out to be incomprehension, and walked out with me to the taxi stand. That no taxis were waiting was another clue that things weren't normal. While we stood, not sure of what to do next, a mule-drawn cart pulled up. The driver studied the paper, mutely shook his head, and directed his mule over to someone else.

I was about to set off on foot when a car—an American Model-T Ford—drove up. This driver, who kept looking over his shoulder, asked me in French where I wanted to go. To my reply, he said, "What do you want to go here for? All gone." The car stalled. He pressed the starter, and it chugged unhappily back into life; lousy gas, I figured. It was then that I noticed the air was gray and smoke filled. At the time I blamed the car.

"All gone," he repeated. "Where do you want to go?"

To my hesitant "Are you sure?" he spat out the window, then said a few words to the old man, who muttered and shook his fists at nothing in particular.

"You see. He says very bad. I'll take you to the hotel. Twelve piastres."

"Which hotel? Where?"

"The Victoria." The driver inclined his head in a roughly northerly direction. This was reassuring. Not only was the venerable inn still standing, but the driver, like all Damascenes when I'd been here before, had assumed that foreigners wished to stay nowhere else. I hated to disappoint him, but I didn't want to go to the Victoria.

"Take me to the Citadel. I'll find my way from there."

"Come, I take you to the hotel. Ten piastres."

I should go on my own, I thought. I'll be able to find the place. But what if they were right? Then what? I thought of George Samad, who had helped me with the purchase in the first place. His office was close to the Victoria. If he was still there.

"Okay," I agreed. "Hotel Victoria, ten piastres." He put the car in gear and revved the motor, again checking around as though avoiding someone.

I got in, then the porter slid in after me and grinned. It looked like I had just hired myself a dragoman. The car, which again had been on the verge of stalling, erupted into life. "Twelve piastres," the driver shouted as we took off, gesturing that the old man was the reason for the extra charge.

Much had changed. A broad boulevard now paralleled the Barada River, and military vehicles were squeezing out donkeys,

DAMAS (Syrie) - Grande Rue et Vue du Grand Hôtel Victoria

Barada

Hôtel Victoria

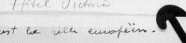

...est la ville européen.

Marche Ali Basha Merjé

12. DAMAS - Le Sérail

Sharia Derviche

merjé

carts, and pedestrians. There were many new buildings. Heading north toward the river, we passed one of them, an oddly becoming European/Arabian concoction. I pointed to it. "Gare du Hijaz," the driver said. "For the train to Mecca," he added. At the approach of a truckload of soldiers, he abruptly turned off the street. When the truck went by, he backed up and we resumed our way. To my puzzled look, he patted the steering wheel. "I keep her, *insh'allah*," he said. I gathered that the army was requisitioning private citizens' cars.

He dropped us off in front of a sign announcing "Olympia Dancing." Except for the addition of this nightclub, the Victoria looked the same, dilapidated and barnlike. The porter and I stood on the road, mutely staring at each other. Since he didn't look like he was going to go away, I stuck out my hand and introduced myself. He looked at my outstretched hand for a moment, then broke into a grin, touched my fingers lightly, then thumped his chest, announcing his name, Ahmed Mustafa at-Tawil. I wondered what the devil I was going to do with a dragoman, not to mention one who neither spoke nor read English or French. Funny, I believe it was the last time I ever questioned his presence.

We headed east to the Sérail, the city's main square. Its name had been changed to Merjé a few years before (and would be changed again a few years later), but I still thought of it by its old name. As I regained my bearings, I became more confident, but this pluck was quickly eroded by the sight of barbed wire and sandbags. Sentries posted around the square were checking papers and turning people away. Fortunately, Samad's building was situated before the blockade. His name and office number, engraved onto a plaque at the entrance, directed us to the second floor, where we found a young man vigorously pounding papers with a rubber stamp. I handed him my card and asked to speak

23

to Samad. He frowned over the empty page of an appointment book, turned and walked into an inner office, and shut the door. I heard bits of a muffled one-sided conversation, then he looked out and asked me my business.

"Bait Katib, 1914," I replied. It occurred to me that Samad, even now in the midst of a revolt, was reachable with a simple call. It had been a matter of pride for him to be one of the first individuals in Damascus to be on the 'phone.

The clerk emerged, indicating that we should take seats on an uncomfortable-looking wooden bench. While we waited, Ahmed shot short glottal bursts at the clerk, getting noncommittal grunts in return, while I fidgeted and tried to keep myself from imagining the worst by aiming my frantic thoughts on the benign memory of George Samad. My initial admiration for him flooded back as I remembered his help and advice. Except for sending him a postcard or two to advise him of my delayed return, I hadn't kept in touch. He had written when Nasim Katib died; otherwise he was as lax a correspondent as I.

I remembered him as being a tall man and was trying to picture how he might have changed when I heard footsteps and wheezing ascending the stairs. Then a corpulent, graying George Samad entered the office, to all appearances an even more imposing figure than before. He towered above our low perch and stared at me quizzically.

"Julian Beaufort? Bait Katib?" His words ended on a high note, as if he did not believe he'd heard correctly.

I stood up, nodded, and smiled. I saw that he had really put on weight. His fingers had become childishly plump, jowls poked out from the sides of his well-trimmed still-black beard, the lines spreading out from the corners of his eyes were puddled, rather than etched. The overall effect added to the natural warmth and welcome in his smile, which was further enhanced by a gold incisor sparkling in what had once been a mouthful of all-white teeth.

Autour de la place principale de Damas, le 23 octobre : nos troupes continuent les travaux de défense, tandis que les habitants déménagent.

Finally, he remembered me and grasped my arms. I was like a rag doll in his grip. "You're the gentleman who bought the house from Nasim Katib," he bellowed, giving me a shake. "How long have you been in Damascus? How have you been withstanding the troubles? Why have you waited before coming to see me?"

"I just arrived. Today."

"But, my God," he exploded, "why now?"

"I'm going to move in, finally."

"And what makes you think it's still there? Don't you know what has happened?"

"Is it that bad?" I asked reluctantly. I didn't want to hear.

"Bad? Bad?" he cried. "It could not be worse." He glanced at his watch. "Come, I'll show you." Then he noticed Ahmed. "Who is this?" he asked but without waiting for a reply spoke directly to the porter. They shouted at each other, then Samad shook his head and said, "Bah, if you wanted a guide you should have come directly here. You don't need an idiot who can't even carry a lady's purse." He pointed to my valise. "Leave that. We'll be back soon."

"No, I'll bring it," I said.

"As you wish." He shrugged his shoulders. Following the notary's rapid pace, Ahmed and I rushed down the stairs and out onto the street. We neatly avoided the blockaded square. George panted as he talked: about the lack of taxis, they

25

Citadelle

Suq al-Hamadiyya

↑ Sidi 'amud / Bab al-Jabiyya

were commandeered to carry soldiers; the lack of petrol, it was siphoned off by the military; the barbed wire and soldiers, they were hired thugs, no less. The curfews, the constant demand for identification, the noise from the low-flying planes. The bombs.

"Look!" He pointed to a man on foot, struggling with a large cabinet. "People are moving their belongings piece by piece. And where are they going, I ask?"

I commented that the trams were still running, at which Samad erupted, "First you think you can move into a house that probably no longer exists, then you are surprised that a streetcar is functioning!"

"Not surprised. Pleased. Look, M. Samad—"

"You were calling me George in 1914, Julian."

"George." I smiled. It was like picking up where we had left off. "When did you last see Bait Katib?"

Before he could reply, an armored car screeched to a halt in front of us. I nearly collapsed. No amount of time could erase that pure reflex of fear. George stood calmly as though waiting for a simple traffic jam to clear; then when the soldiers had hopped out and rushed off, we made our way around the car and continued on. My legs were wobbly, but George's composure was reassuring.

He didn't answer my question, instead asking if I had heard that Nasim Katib had died. I reminded him that he had written. Then he told me that Muna Katib had also died, a few years ago, of a cancer, he thought.

This was scarcely the time or place to reflect on the sad news, but I was taken aback. I asked, "What about the daughter?

76. Damaskus. Eingang zum Suk Hamidie Bazar.

Did she get married?" But he knew nothing of her, nor if the house was occupied.

As we neared the Suq al-Hamadiyya, I could make out the market's distinctive entrance with its half-barrel vaulted roof, unchanged except for the Senegalese sentries, tall, black, and terribly out of place. The haze, so noticeable at the train station, was even thicker here. When I asked George about it, all he said was, "You'll see. Now," he eyed me, "I don't suppose you have a *laissez-passer*?" He shook his head. "No, of course not. Oh well, what kind of trouble can we get into?" We bypassed the soldiers and the main entrance, ducked into a doorway a few yards down, cut through a warehouse, then came out into a back lane. From there we made our way into the darkened market.

Our route took us partway down the bazaar. Some of the merchants had boarded up their shops; others were struggling to maintain a semblance of normalcy. There were no customers, as far as I could see.

At the second junction we turned right and headed into a smoldering cemetery of charred houses. Blackened beams and posts in skeletal poses; window frames crazily angled, slipping where the walls below them had crumbled away; fallen-in ceilings, sweeping down to the ground like heavy velvet drapes; bricks stacked in senselessly neat piles. The still-erect façade of one building, now a new entrance for the back wall of a building across the lane. The few passersby were grim-faced, in shock. The farther we went into this hell, the greater my dismay.

DAWN

A RAY OF LIGHT shining through the shutters broke Julian's concentration. It was morning. As he considered what he'd written, he saw that he'd spent more time dreaming and doodling, but he was exhausted, so he stood up, stretched, and turned off the lamp. When he left the study, he was so lost in thought that he couldn't have seen the slight, shadowy woman who had come, some time during the night, to watch him from the dark corner of the room.

Asilah

FRIDAY, MAY 25TH, 1945

MORNING

AFTER JULIAN LEFT, Asilah sat motionless, resting her chin in her hands. This study, where her father had worked, was her favorite room. It was his pots that Julian filled with ink, his pens that Julian wrote with, and, until it had finally run out, his paper that Julian wrote on.

She'd overheard Julian and the strangers discussing Bait Katib; there wasn't much that happened in the house that she missed. How was it possible that someone else could think they had a claim on the house? No matter what she thought of Julian's ownership of it, he had bought it legitimately with her father's complete approval. No one else had a right to it. And what did Julian propose to do about this claim? She went to the desk— nearly tripping over a stack of books on the floor—with the intention of reading through the papers the men had left with him. But when she saw the notebook lying open on the desk, she flipped through its pages, back to front, and forgot the document. She reached the beginning of the book and reversed directions, reading slowly, as her knowledge of English was meager.

1945 already. Time had gone so quickly. It seemed as though Julian had just moved in. That he had done so twenty years ago was almost inconceivable. She looked at her hands. Are these the hands of a forty-nine-year-old? She searched out her reflection in the brass lampshade. Is this the hair, the eyes, the mouth of a forty-nine-year-old? She shook her head in disbelief.

She smiled at Julian's description of Damascus, its narrow streets, the beautiful houses, and of her own home, Bait Katib.

But her smile disappeared at his account of the war. "I had no idea," she murmured. She shivered when she read of his arrival in Damascus. His words brought back the terror of October 1925, when the bombs fell and the buildings round her caught fire.

Although there had been fighting outside Damascus earlier that year between the Druze and the French, no one, herself included, believed that the troubles would come any closer. But the anger that had erupted in the city when the duplicitous Lord Balfour had shown his face! Who could have predicted that thousands would march in protest!

Still, the delusion of peace persisted. Until October, that is, after the French destroyed several villages and paraded captured rebels—living and dead—in the Place du Sérail. From that moment on, Damascus was poised to fight.

Asilah herself lived in the midst of open hostility. Conversations with neighbors in the street, once energetic, voluble, became hushed and clandestine, drying up like water in a summer heat at the approach of anyone suspicious, whether it was an informer, a soldier, even a tourist, though tourists were rare, as they were by then fearfully avoiding the region. Her friends whispered nervously to her of their brothers, young men all, who were hiding out in the Ghouta, the orchards around Damascus, armed to the teeth and ready to strike.

She was sickened by the rumors: that the French were about to unleash their mercenaries to slaughter, rape, and pillage. Or that certain Damascus officials had sold off their city for a handful of gold and safe haven in Europe. She believed none of these lies yet couldn't deny that the military buildup portended something awful.

The actual attack caught her off guard. At first she thought an earthquake had hit. A thunderous clap had been followed by objects tumbling to the floor; an especially heavy book struck her hand hard on its descent. She recalled watching it land awkwardly, its pages twisting and bending under its own weight. She saw that the binding had torn at the spine and that the pages had creased. And she was left with this image of the book hurting her and hitting the floor. And that it had hurt her and was damaged was all that mattered, because it saved her from thinking about what was going on outside.

In shock, she kept staring at the book on the floor, until the unearthly wail of missiles penetrated, first distant whines, gelling into shrieks. She had never before heard such sounds, yet she knew immediately what they were. The next explosion was farther away. She sagged in relief, realizing only then how rigidly she'd been holding herself. An incredible scream followed, close, so close it hurt her ears. The stink of the bomb seared her nostrils, burned in its passage to her lungs. She braced herself again. This time it was as though the blast tore the house apart. Windows on the upper floor shattered; more books crashed to the floor.

She fell on her knees, shielding herself with her thin arms. After a moment of silence, she made herself get up to see what must have been the end of the world.

The neighboring house had caught fire. Tongues of flame burst up over the top of the wall. She strained to catch sounds of life but heard nothing save the howls of a trapped dog. She covered her ears as the baying subsided to a whimper. When she finally lowered her hands, there was only the crackling of the fire.

The coming night had further fed her fears and drove her to try to escape. If escape appeared possible, it was a deception caused by warm light dancing in the darkening sky. The house was about to succumb to a blaze that seemed to consume the entire city. She put on a thick robe to shield her from flames and stuffed a handful of gold coins in her pocket. At the last second, she grabbed a piece of her father's artwork.

Smoke filled the lane, obscuring all beyond her reach. A terror-stricken man swam silently out of the haze and nearly collided with her. He swerved just in time and, without a word, disappeared again. Flashes of red punctuated the darkness. Shouting—disembodied Arab and French voices, at times low and garbled, at times loud and clear—reverberated through the streets, pummeling her from all sides.

Her disorientation was complete. She had no idea which way to turn, whether to run or to just collapse and wait to die. Then she heard footsteps and turned to face the direction they seemed to be coming from. They were level with her before she could identify her neighbors, the Majids, so shrouded were they in their hooded cloaks. "Come with us," they shouted as they ran past, holding out their arms as though to grab her. Intent on joining them, she moved forward, but a burst of shelling wrenched the ground from beneath her feet.

Shaken, she picked herself up and ran a few steps when her foot struck a soft bundle. It was Selim, the Majids' youngest son, who must have fallen without his parents' noticing. "Wait!" she screamed, but they'd already turned the corner. She put her hand under the boy's head and raised it slightly. "Selim!" she cried, shaking him. "Get up!" She ran her hand across his forehead and sobbed. She struggled to pick him up. A lifeless sack, he was heavy in her arms, but she managed to carry him to the door. Then another bomb exploded behind her. The force flung her into a semiconscious void, crackling with the pulsating shocks of the detonations. As she fell a hail of machine-gun fire ricocheted off the wall above her, spraying her with chips of stone.

When she came to, her first thought was one of wonder that she was still alive. She'd been awakened, perhaps by the rising sun or perhaps by the deep silence that had temporarily blanketed the city. Then, remembering the boy, she looked around for him, but he had vanished.

In no state to worry about what had happened to him, she crawled to the door, chancing a quick look behind her. The sight of blood staining the cobblestones where she had lain sent her scurrying in a panic into the house. She slammed, then locked the door.

The front of her robe was stiff with dried blood. Was it hers or Selim's? Her arms and hands and face smarted from bruises and scrapes, and her forehead burned. Her torso ached and, when she tried to stand up, stabbing pains shot across her back. Everything round her went black.

She awoke to renewed gunfire and shelling. Frantic banging on her door—supplications for refuge that she closed her ears to—subsided quickly, clearing the air for an unearthly pandemonium surging past on the other side of the wall: the trample of feet, the desperate dragging of possessions, the piercing cries, the hoarse shouts. The calls to prayer cutting through the chaos heightened the inconceivable grotesqueness of the situation.

I'll never leave again, she swore. If I am to die, it will only be within Bait Katib's walls. She couldn't shake the image of Selim Majid nor the certainty that he was dead when she held him in her arms.

When the thunder of the bombardment stopped that evening, she dragged herself up the stone stairs to the second floor and looked out through what had been a window to the wasted city around her. Where were the houses of her neighbors? Why, she could see all the way through to the painted mural in the grand reception room in the house of the Quwatlis, the only feature, it appeared, of that magnificent house still standing. The world outside was beyond her imagination. She turned her back on it.

It was good that Julian was writing this out, she thought. Such a testimony will most eloquently make his case. But I must add my own plea, for the courts will be sympathetic if they believe that a member of the immediate family considers him to be the legitimate owner. She took up a pen, dipped it into the ink pot, touched the nib to the paper, and began to shape a letter. Then hesitated. Under the pressure of her hand, the nib bent slightly, releasing a pool of ink around the first stroke. The page was half-filled with Julian's neat printing, his words in staccato roman letters, against which her Arabic script would clash. In an instant, she closed the book, turned it over, opened it again to what had been its last page, and began writing, from back to front and from right to left. With all of the blank pages between them, he wouldn't realize that she had filled the end of his book with her beginning. Not until he needed to know.

الكن كيف ؟ ليس لدي سلاح غير سيف
الزينة يستطيع اي رجل ان يسلبه من
يدي بسهولة . ولو صرخت اليهم ان
يذهبوا بعيدا، يمكن ان يصمموا اكثر على
دخول البيت . وبالرغم هذا فتحت فمي
اريد ان اصرخ الآن ايد وان الخوف قد
خنق صوتي .

واخيرا انفتح القفل صارخا بصوت معدني
عالي ، تبعه صوت ضرب الصد ور انتصارا.
واتخذت خطوات بسيطة بعيدة عن
الباب ، و وقفت بحجرة انظر اليه ينفتح ببطأ
ليد عن ضجيج الشارع الدخول . واحذت
المدينة تحتل ملجئي، المدينة التي
احببتها طيلة حياتي . والشوارع التي
العبت فيها ايام طفولتي ، اوالاشياء
التي اصبحت متعفنة ومقززة ، كل هذه
جاءت لتحتل ملجئي . ومشيت ببطأ
يشابه في سرعته انفتاح الباب ، ولجأت
الى ظلام الممربين لبحري، ومن ثم الى داخل
احداهما حيث سيكون بامكاني ان
اراقب الدخلاء من دون ان يروني .

تذكرت
ابي فقط
اللصوص الذين هجموا
"بيي كاتب الدفاع عن
ضد
على البيت الذين هجموا
عام ١٨٦٠. لقد كان ابي
الشاب الوحيد خلال عصيان
رجل شجاع من اخوان
ذاك الوقت . كيف
له امرأة. كيف لي . انا
المرأة الوحيدة الشابة
التي ترعرعت على الكتب
والموسيقى ان ادافع ضد
العساكر او اللصوص ؟

The day Julian arrived

It is as if it happened just yesterday, and it was a day much like yesterday, change brought by the arrival of three strangers. This change was heralded by a rasping screech shooting through the air, a screech loud enough to wake the dead. With the horrifying fighting that had been taking place, the sound nearly tore my heart in two, and for a moment I trembled too much to move. When my nerves finally steadied themselves, I ran over to the door where I could see the tip of a key wiggling in the rusty lock. Mutterings became audible, voices of the men wrestling with the key's other end.

Why try that lock? I wondered. It was for the oversize main door, into which a smaller one had been set, and hadn't been opened for at least a decade. There wasn't even a key for it anymore. As befitted my agitated mind, worrying about this detail was irrational, considering the more pressing question of *who* was trying to get in and *why*. For reassurance, I grasped my own key, safe in my pocket, a Yale, the lock for which my father had installed on the smaller door in 1914, shortly before he died. The key's increasingly frenzied movements tore me out of this futile reverie.

I held my breath as the corroded bolt loosened. More voices could be heard, low pitched but voluble, closer. Someone banged on the door. It could only be soldiers, intent on destroying the little that I had left. In a minute they'd be swarming through the place with their machine guns and grenades. I had to do something to stop them. I threw myself against the door, as if my powerless body alone was strong enough to hold them back. I would not relive that horrible night. I would stop them with any means.

But how? I had no weapons, save for an ornamental sword, which any man could easily wrest from me. I remembered my father's vivid stories about defending Bait Katib against looters who had attacked the house during the bloody revolt of 1860. Only my father had been a youth then, a brave young man, with strong brothers. How could I—a lone young woman who had been nurtured on books and music—defend myself against soldiers or thieves? And if I yelled at them to go away, it would make them all the more determined to get in. Still, I opened my mouth, ready to cry out, and found that fear had strangled my voice.

The lock finally gave way with a metallic shriek, over which triumphant cheers burst. I stepped away from the door and stood, petrified, watching it creep open as the babble from the street poured in. The very city that I had loved all my life, the very streets that had been my nursery, my playground, these things that had become foul and hideous and that I now strove to keep out, were invading my sanctuary. I paced myself with the door's slow swing, then I slipped into the darkness of the passageway, and then to one of the rooms off the courtyard, where I would be able to observe the intruders without being seen.

A bearded, elderly man peered into the courtyard, then stepped into the open, turned around, and waved. Another man, also with a beard but middle-aged and wearing a European suit, entered. He unfolded himself as he emerged from the passageway, proving to be massive in both height and width. A much younger and slighter man, clean shaven, in a suit as well, and carrying a small valise, came after him. Their head-gear distinguished them further. The old man wore a loosely wound, dirty-looking turban; the middle-aged one, a fez; and the youngest, a wide-brimmed felt hat. They didn't look as though they had come to pillage the place, nor were they soldiers. I waited to see what they would do.

More people pushed their way in. I recognized among them

the faces of my neighbors who hadn't fled or been killed. A palpable tremor shook the crowd, but at the word *Ingalizi*, it became noticeably calmer.

Clutching a large key, the old man gestured broadly about the courtyard and solemnly turned to the young man. *"Haadha baitak!"* he announced. Gasps and whispers resounded, the loudest of which must have been mine.

The younger man frowned, then asked, in French. "Did he say, 'This is your house?'"

"Well done," responded the large man. "And so it is! Congratulations!"

"Ma maison," the younger man repeated, "my home. My home in Damascus." He sighed deeply and, from the shadows of my hiding place, I could see his smile.

What were they talking about? This was *my* home.

They strolled to the fountain in the center of the courtyard. The younger one took off his hat, smoothed his straight brown hair, rubbed the back of his head, then balanced the hat on the fountain's rim. We all watched his every move. I took a deep breath and resolved to walk out to confront them. They have no right to be here, I told myself.

Just then shouting broke out, and Najwa, our maid, burst through the crowd. The quarter's grapevine was as efficient as ever. She pushed aside her veil to show a very red and angry face and demanded to be told what was going on, all the while glowering at the intruders. The younger man appeared confused and concerned. The large one was passive; he was the one to be careful of. With a mere glance, he signaled the porter to respond. The porter and Najwa hurled insults and accusations at each other with equal enthusiasm. I urged her on. She would get rid of them, and then I would come out.

At that moment, Najwa cupped her hands and yelled out my name, but I was determined to wait until the men had gone.

"She is calling Asilah Katib," I heard the porter say, in Arabic.

"George," said the young man, "Asilah Katib, that's the daughter."

Suddenly, I remembered the man who had bought the house the year before my father died. Could this be him? I searched my memory for the name, but it was gone.

Najwa called again, then stormed off into the room closest to her.

I should have gone to her. But I stood rooted to the spot and, having hesitated—even though for only a moment—thoroughly lost my nerve.

"She is looking for her mistress," the porter continued.

I watched her plod up the staircase and reappear on the walkway. Leaning over the balustrade, she shouted down.

The middle-aged man translated. "She says this house is private property and we should leave. Ahmed tells her she should leave. She says it belongs to her mistress. Ahmed says show us your mistress."

The man sounded irritated. "She says show me your papers. Ahmed says again, show us your mistress. She says show me . . . O, give me patience." He called up to her, "Yes, yes, tell us something important! And please come back down!"

I slunk over to the window. What harm would come if I were to walk out? The stranger sounded reasonable. If he were the same man, my father had certainly liked him. But what if he kicks me out? Would I be allowed to take anything? How would I pay for a new home? If it weren't for the big man, I might have gone out, right then and there. Between Najwa and me, we could have persuaded the younger one to leave. But this George looked as though he could evict his own mother. I decided he was from Beirut.

"Do you have the deed here, Julian?" George asked.

41

Julian. That was the name. He *was* the same man. I remembered he was English, or at least spoke English, though he and George were conversing in French. But Julian what?

The man called Julian unfolded a piece of paper and handed it to George, who scanned through it. "Here," he said, pointing to it, "Nasim Katib."

My father's name rippled through the crowd. The porter gestured for the document and haltingly read out its contents. His words brought back every detail of the sale of the house, including the young man's full name, Julian Beaufort.

I hadn't paid attention at the time, but then, having just become engaged, I was preoccupied. The first I'd even heard that the house was for sale was when there had been a flurry of activity one morning. My mother and Najwa were cleaning even more than usual, and they put out the best china in the salon reserved for important guests. As she dusted the table, my mother announced the plan.

"What?!" I cried. "You've said nothing to me! Nothing! You can't sell it. What about me?"

My mother's look shamed me.

"Sold to whom?" My voice was again calm, but inside I was appalled.

"To the foreigner."

"What foreigner?"

"Asilah! You know perfectly well. The Englishman who is staying with us, Sayyid Beaufort."

"But why?"

"Because your father has decided the house will not be so important when you go live with Tariq."

"But what about you two? Do you need money?" I knew exactly how much my wedding and dowry cost. I was sure my father could easily afford it.

My mother had given me a reassuring hug. "Don't worry

about us," she said. "We aren't going to move out right away. This foreigner buys the house now. He thinks he will come back soon, but he won't until after the war is over—if the war ever ends—and then he will live here."

"But why a foreigner? Why not family? And what will you do when he makes you leave?"

My mother had suddenly looked far older than her fifty years. She must have known my father hadn't many more months to live, but neither of them ever said a word. They didn't want to spoil my happiness.

"I don't think we have to worry," she said. "Perhaps it will be a very long war, in any event. And your father believes that Sayyid Beaufort will love Bait Katib more than anyone else in the family. Even more than you."

I was exasperated with her complacence and mortified that my father could think so little of my regard for the family house, after all it had never belonged to anyone but a Katib. I pursued another angle: "What if Tariq and I move back here?" I asked.

"You don't understand families," my mother had sighed. "You'll belong to another soon. You'll forget about Bait Katib."

"I won't," I cried. "This house means everything to me. I *want* Tariq to live here."

"But you will be living in a newer house in Salhiyya."

"Only at first, to keep the peace with his mother. I'll convince him that we belong in Bait Katib, and then we'll come back."

"Not anymore, I'm afraid. The house is as good as sold. And besides, Tariq's family expects you to live with them. You will see how strong tradition is. Just because your father and I let you do as you want, you think you can get away with anything!"

I sulked, I whined, I cajoled, I threatened to call off the wedding. I promised to do whatever was necessary to restore my father's faith in my desire to keep Bait Katib. But it was still sold to the foreigner, whom I now hated with a passion. I avoided him, a difficult task since he was staying with us.

Anyway, on this day, a notary had come. Perhaps it was even this man George. Everyone sat in the salon, drinking coffee. Except me. I had boldly shaken hands, then left. As if I didn't care what happened to my home when, in truth, I was nauseated and despondent. While I was absent, the papers were signed, and the house no longer belonged to us. After two hundred and ten years, our family was homeless. But true to my mother's word, the foreigner went away with his papers, and we lived as though he didn't exist.

My father's death the following spring was a dreadful blow. But the loss of my father and the remorse I felt over the sale of the house were eased by my love for my husband. Tariq was near to my own age and worked for the Banque Ottomane. We had an apartment in his parents' large and very modern house in Salhiyya. My mother had been right. In no time, I had forgotten all about my dreams of returning to Bait Katib with its decrepit walls and claustrophobic history. I loved this new life and was turning away from the old. I even begged my mother to move in with us, as it would save me the frequent trips back. Of course, she refused.

And what a long war it was, so long that I had forgotten about the foreigner, who had been no more than a boy. Was this really the same person? I stared through the lattice-screened window, concentrating on his features. He had a pleasant but thin face. His hands were meant for someone taller, larger. I was struck by his tranquility.

My attention drifted back to the discussion still taking place in the courtyard.

"Maybe she's out shopping or visiting?" Julian was asking.

Najwa began to cry. She was breaking my heart.

George spoke. "We just walked through miserable streets, full of danger, not a place for you, not a place for me, not a place for Asilah Katib. What would she be doing out shopping or gossiping? However, perhaps she has gone to Salhiyya or Beirut. She was surely afraid of staying here alone."

Yes, I was afraid. But it was better here than out in the open.

Throughout their endless speculations as to my whereabouts, I immersed myself in memories. When Julian returned to Europe in 1914, my awareness of the rest of the world left with him. His war barely touched us, though there were more soldiers in the streets, but in Syria this was nothing new. Famine devastated the poorer quarters of the city, but our real burden had been the Turks, and when they were evacuated and Faysal marched into Damascus, we all renewed our hopes for the future. However, the war's end brought us only more shortages and unbearable overcrowding.

That's when the changes really started. Rumors swept through the bazaars. The Ottomans were bankrupt; the English were taking over Palestine. No one knew if that meant they wanted Syria as well, or if we would be controlled by the French, who already had the railway concession and other businesses. The rumors transformed into fact. Europe surveyed the Levant, and then divided us up, as if we were theirs to do with what they wished. England took Palestine and Mesopotamia, and France got us.

Not that I cared. Not at the time.

I heard my name again and listened more closely.

"But Asilah was married, wasn't she?" Julian was asking. "What about her husband?"

"Tariq was killed," I answered, my eyes burning.

It didn't matter that no one heard me; they all knew one version or another of the story; a dozen voices fought to tell it. "Her husband was killed," they chorused. "By the French," said

45

وكما لو كنت أريد
أن اطمأن نفسي،
بحثت في حقيبتي.
عن مفتاح قفل الباب
الصغير الذي ركبه
والدي عام ١٩١٤ بوقت
قصير قبل وفاته.

الآن محاولة الرجال
على الجانب الثاني
هزت أعصابي
وأصبحت عاجزة
عن إيجاد مفتاح
ذلك القفل.

one man, pointing his finger accusingly at Julian. "No, by the Druze," said another, "during the uprising." "In 1920," said a third, "after Faysal left. Just like that," he clapped his hands together sharply, "by a stray bullet."

"Someone shot him," I added, "in the middle of Straight Street. It was doubtless the revenge of a businessman who lost money in the Ottoman collapse." My tears had not yet dried. After he was buried, I retreated to Bait Katib. No longer the wife of Tariq Qani, I chose to become Asilah Katib once more.

Najwa spoke next. "She moved back to her mother, who was ailing."

My mother's illness. Much of my inheritance had gone to pay for us to travel to Europe to consult with doctors. The rest was spent on hospitals, food, and medicine during the last two years of her life.

And when my mother died, I closed the door on my past and my future. The house was all I had, and I forgot that I no longer owned it.

"Her mother died," I heard Najwa say. Then, shifting the topic, as only Najwa could, she said, "The big door is not to be opened." From under her robes she pulled out her own Yale key. "For the little door," she snapped, waving it in the men's faces. "I buy food and clean. I will do this until *she* tells me to stop." I knew then that Najwa had given up. Julian Beaufort would be staying.

"When did you last see her?" George asked.

Najwa made a face at him. "Before the troubles."

"But that was over two weeks ago. You haven't been here since?"

"I am here now." She folded her arms and stared defiantly. "And I have brought food, though, by God, it is difficult to find anything. It cost me forty-five piastres." She turned around and called out "M'hamm'd!" A small boy, dragging a wicker basket,

46

threaded his way through the bystanders. "Here is her food for this week." I stared after the boy; I was starving. "M'hamm'd!" Najwa pointed to the kitchen. He ran into the house and emerged a minute later, the basket empty.

Resignation was heavy in Najwa's voice, "My heart tells me she's here. She'll come out when she wants to, *insh'allah*."

Najwa had completely failed to dislodge the foreigner, but knowing how much she would suffer if she didn't find me, I decided to walk out into the courtyard, then held back, yet again filled with doubts and misgivings. How would this help me keep my home? Would I be forced to go and live with Najwa in her wretched little apartment with her invalid husband and her rough sons?

Worse still, my belly again churned at the memory of the terrifying night. Nothing could convince me that it was over. Tanks still rumbled nearby. Soldiers still marched past. Nighttime still brought shooting and explosions. Devastation was still visible through my windows. I had only to recall my revulsion at the opening of the door a few minutes earlier to know I couldn't go out there.

The crowd lost interest. One by one, they departed, leaving only the three men and Najwa, her fists defiantly fixed upon her hips.

"You are welcome in my home tonight, Julian," announced George. "Then you can move here tomorrow morning."

"Go with him," I prompted. I was not only famished, but I was cold and cramped.

"No," said Julian. "Thanks all the same. Now that I'm here, I couldn't possibly leave."

George told Najwa that Monsieur Beaufort was moving into the house. Tears again rolled down her cheeks. "He'll frighten her," she spat out between sobs.

I yanked on my hair. "Go away, all of you," I moaned.

يوم وصل جوليان

كان هذا الحدث كما انه حصل بالامس والفارق هو وصول ثلاثة غرباء. وسبق هذا الحدث صوت قصف ناري حاد في الهواء كاد ان يفيق الميت من سباته الابدي. ومزق هذا الصوت قلبي خاصة انه جاء في وقت يسوده قتال مخيف. واللحظات اهتز بدني بشدة حيث تجمدت ولم استطع الحراك. وبعد ما خفت الصدمة على اعصابي، تجرأت وذهبت الى الباب حيث رأيت طرف مفتاح في قفل الباب. وبدى لي ان بعض الرجال على الجانب الثاني يتهامسون حول امر فتح الباب.

واستغربت لامرهم وهم يحاولون فتح قفل الباب الرئيسي الكبير الذي لم يستعمل منذ عقد من السنين، حتى ان مفتاحه ضاع منذ زمن طويل، في الوقت الذي كان هناك قفل اخر على باب اصغر شفت في الباب الكبير. وكان من الغريب ان ينشغل بالي في امر القفل، وهو تفكير غير معقول في هذا الظرف، بينما كان علي ان افكر بالامر الاهم وهو من

وهويوم لم يختلف عن الامس كثيرا

The porter reassured Najwa that the Sayyid would be most civil to me, at such time as I returned, God willing, and that he would certainly continue to pay Najwa for her splendid services—including the forty-five piastres—and did it truly matter for whom she cleaned or brought food? She agreed to come back the next day to formalize the arrangements. As she adjusted her veil and prepared to leave, I envied her bravery and wept for the loss of my own.

George suggested that they go eat. Then they looked in dismay toward the door.

"Do you think we really broke the lock?" Julian asked.

"Without a doubt," George answered. "Too bad we didn't get that key off of the maid. Then we could have rigged up something to secure the big door."

I couldn't hear Julian's reply.

George laughed. "Well, maybe she brought something edible. You should have asked her to cook us dinner. Do you suppose there's electricity?" Night was fully upon us, and the house was dark.

"There was in 1914," Julian replied. His awkward shuffling echoed round the courtyard. I listened to their footfalls as they made their way to the kitchen and imagined them running their hands up the walls, grasping for cords that might be dangling from the ceiling. I, too, crossed the courtyard, to where I could eavesdrop undetected.

A match flared, momentarily illuminating the doorway. Suddenly a child's voice broke through the darkness. "*Ya fendim*. Where are you?" It was Muhammad.

"Over here," replied George. "Does this house have electric light?"

"Yes, *ya fendim*." A shadowy Muhammad, carrying a tray laden with a teapot and glasses, slid with a cat's assurance into the kitchen. "Here, *ya fendim*." Light flooded the room, and I moved out of its reach. The bulb buzzed like a fly and flickered weakly. The boy skittered back through the courtyard and vanished.

I slumped against the wall and listened to the preparation of the meal: chopping, boiling, sizzling. George had lit the brazier and was grilling vegetables. The agonizing fragrance of peppers and oil wafted out into the courtyard. I distracted myself by eavesdropping. I couldn't catch every word of Julian's hard-to-follow French but understood that he overflowed with plans for the house.

At one point he came out into the courtyard and called, "Ahmed." Not getting any response, he walked back into the kitchen.

When George left, Julian explored each room. Even when he couldn't find a light switch, he fingered tapestries, stroked furniture, and peered into cupboards. I glared at him from my hidden vantage points when he rifled through papers in my father's study and when he opened drawers in my mother's desk. Something made him nervous—maybe he sensed my presence—for he frequently paused and checked over his shoulder.

I held my breath when he entered my bedroom on the second floor. I had taken to leaving the mattress unrolled on the floor. And more than that, I had left all manner of clothes scattered about. He would know this was my room; he would see my things.

However, he simply looked at the shattered window, pushed around the broken glass that I hadn't bothered to sweep up, then left, shutting the door behind him. He went back down to the courtyard where he retrieved his valise and took it into the *qa'a*, the reception room, at the far end. From the shelter of a screened window, I watched him rearrange the divan to make it more comfortable to sleep on. He laid down in his coat, it was that cold. I took off to the kitchen and quietly picked at scraps left from dinner.

My mind boiled over with ideas of how to regain my house, but none of them made any sense. If I confronted him and he put me out, where would I go? I couldn't afford a new place to live. And even if he allowed me to stay, how could I? It would shame me to live in a house with a man who was not a relative. If I forced him to leave, he could return with policemen and have me thrown out, even worse, have all of my belongings confiscated. Perhaps I could intimidate him into leaving, but what threats could I make? And besides, what if he then sold the house to someone else? A family with children, servants? Every angle put me in a terrible position, giving me no choice but to make the best of it for the time being, by surreptitiously sharing the house with him, attuning my ear to his movements, and staying one step ahead of him. I crept up the stairs to my room. My decision infused me with a sense of, if not peace then, at least, resolve, and I soon fell asleep.

I woke early the next morning, peeked in on the intruder, who was sleeping soundly, and went to wash up, grateful that the sounds from the streets drowned out the noise of my movements. An alarm clock rang, startling me. This was a sound that had never been heard before in the house. Never had anyone needed a clock to tell them when to get up. I will get rid of the clock, I vowed.

Afternoon

ASILAH SHOOK HERSELF BACK INTO THE PRESENT. How dare she waste time scribbling nonsense about the past when the house needed to be saved? She reached down to where she had seen Julian drop the document and dug it out from under the pile of books and papers that had accumulated during the course of the night. She smoothed it out and skimmed through it to make sure that she hadn't misunderstood. It was all there, just as she had heard. As was the name of the claimant. When she read his name, she understood. Unless she thought of a way to keep it out of his hands, Bait Katib was to be relinquished to her cousin's husband. She'd never met this fellow, but she knew all about his malicious ways. She snorted as she read out his name, Amin, or trustworthy. Trustworthy, indeed.

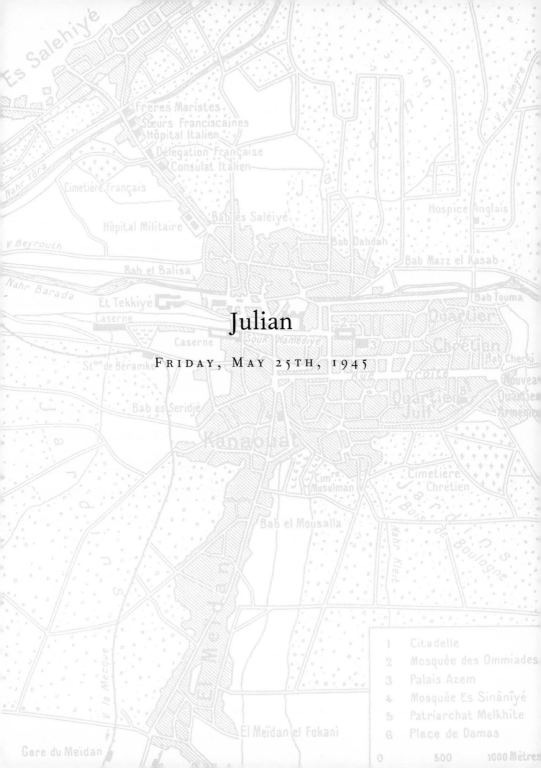

Julian

ٱلحقل فيجده راقدا مستريحا في إصطَبْل نظيف مكنوس من شوش وفي مَعْلَفه ٱلشَّي ، ٱلكثير من ٱلشَّعير ٱلمُغَرْبَل وٱلتّبْن ٱلمُمْتاز .

تَصيحَة ٱلحمار للثور

ففي ذات يوم سمع ٱلرجل ٱلثور وهو يقول للحمار : هنيئا لك ، أنا تعبان وأنت مستريح ، تأكُل ٱلشَّعير مُغَرْبَلا ويخدمونك وفي بعض ٱلأوْقات فقط يَرْكَبُك صاحبك لقضاء حاجته ثم يُرْجِمُك الى مكانك هذا ٱلجميل وأنا دائما للحَرْث وٱلطَّحْن . وقال له ٱلحمار : أدُلُّك على حيلة لتَرْتاح . اذا خَرَجْتَ الى ٱلغَيْط ووضعوا على رَقَبَتِك ٱلنير فَٱرْقُدْ ولا تَقُمْ ولو ضربوك فإن قُمْتَ فَٱرْقُدْ ثانيا فاذا رجعوا بك ووضعوا لك ٱلفول فلا تأكُله كأنّك ضعيف وٱمْتَنِعْ من ٱلأكْل وٱلشُّرب يوما أو يومين أو ثلاثة فإنّك تستريح من

EVENING

JULIAN FROWNED AT THE DOCUMENT now draped over his notebook, then glanced down at the floor where he thought he'd left it. He'd just come into his study, having abandoned a fitful sleep, and was eager to tackle the letter of appeal.

In his mind, the letter was already written a hundred times over, but the moment he put pen to paper, all of his clever phrases evaporated. Hoping to revive them, he began to reread the document but tossed it aside before finishing. With a frustrated sigh, he sat back and thumped the arms of his chair. He pushed the shutter open. Warm evening air filled the room and conspired with the dim light of dusk to undermine his will. It's the lousy sleep, he told himself, I'm too tired. And it's too late to do anything, at any rate, at least until tomorrow. Then he sternly changed his mind.

"May 26th, 1945," he wrote.

To whom does one address such a letter? If George Samad were still in Syria, he'd know. Julian settled on "The Court of Appeals." It could always be changed. The important thing was to establish his arguments.

"I am writing to protest the action taken by—" What was the man's name? Not Katib. This fellow had married into the family. Julian reread the first page, found the name Amin al-Rafiq, and wrote it down. Rafiq doesn't seem like such a bad sort, once you get around the fact that he wants my house, Julian thought, then looked outside. It was pitch-black.

"In regards to the house—" Or should it be "In regards to *my* house"? He started again. "In regards to my house known as Bait Katib, Harat al-Hariqa, Damascus, purchased on the—" Was the purchase date more important than the date when he moved in? He dutifully wrote down both. But maybe the date when he moved in would confuse things. He scratched it out. On the other hand, he must emphasize that he had occupied the house continuously since 1925. He wrote it back in. When the deed was issued should be specified, but there were two, if you counted the revision he'd obtained a few years later. Should he add that, too? Maybe if he referred to how god-awful the house was when he moved in and all he had done to fix it up. The damage to the exterior walls, the fallen roof—, but he could save that for if a right of appeal is granted. *When* a right of appeal is granted.

Shouldn't a lawyer be doing this? He dropped the pen and drummed his fingers on the desk. The house. It had been a shock when he first laid eyes on it, and yet—. His memories, now they'd escaped, wouldn't let him be. He turned to the notebook and recommenced writing in it, avoiding the blob of ink below his last entry.

Miraculously, Bait Katib was still standing, though it had endured a fair amount of shelling, and near the door were horrendous scars, what looked like bullet holes from a machine-gun fusillade.

The key, which I tore from the strap around my neck, was no match for the hopelessly rusty lock. Nasim's vow that with it I would be the only one able to open the door looked pretty unlikely, but we finally succeeded after scraping out the lock with my knife. Once inside, I was relieved to find that the house was very much intact, apart from a ghastly hole in the courtyard wall and another, smaller one in the wall of the second-story summer reception salon. There was also a partially collapsed roof in the room I had slept in eleven years ago and blown-out windows on three sides of the house. Some objects had fallen off shelves but not as many as one might expect.

I don't remember much about the rest of that day. A lively crowd gathered, but otherwise the house was empty. I had assumed—hoped—the family would be there, even though I knew both Nasim and Muna had passed away. As for Asilah, it appeared that she had been living there but had vanished a short time before my arrival.

This was when I met Najwa. She had rushed in and screamed at us, then, to my surprise, agreed to work for me. Since she had long been the Katibs' maid, we would have presumably seen each other in 1914, but neither of us could recollect the other at all. She stayed on only to safeguard the house for Asilah's return and always blamed me for Asilah's absence.

But this is all jumping ahead. Back to November 2nd. As I said, I don't remember much, excited as I was. George shooed off everyone, found us some dinner, then snuck home through the curfew. Where did Ahmed get to that night? I'd lost track of him.

No, I remember, he patrolled the street, because we couldn't get the door shut again. I was mortified to discover him on the threshold the next morning. Mortified that I'd forgotten about him and that he'd done this for me.

So, I was alone that night, except for the powerful feeling of being watched. The next morning I attributed it to a subconscious awareness of Ahmed, but in time I knew it wasn't the only reason.

The first days in the house were a roller-coaster ride of fear of the bombardments and joy with the house. Today, it's the joy that floods my memory. The joy of wending my way round the shady gallery encircling the second floor, of inspecting the kitchen's immense wood-burning oven, and of exploring the grand reception hall, or *qa'a*, as it's called, with its naively painted murals of magical faraway places: panoramas of Constantinople, bird's-eye views of Vienna, gardens at Versailles.

Intriguing, too, were the many cupboards, each perfect snapshots of Nasim, Muna, and Asilah, for all of their effects—clothing, jewelry, books, musical instruments, bric-à-brac—had been left, as though their owners would return any minute. And, because Nasim had been a scribe and calligrapher, examples of his work, representing a king's ransom of words, hung in each room. Thick, black script in Arabic, Persian, and Ottoman Turkish snaked across sheets of parchment, vellum, and silk; borders and motifs were painted in gold and carmine. But the best words of all were the ones I had already been introduced to, those sculpted in plaster on every available inch of the courtyard walls.

Nasim, who had spoken fluent, courtly French, had taken great pains to explain this work to me. It was a history of words, he said, pointing out that his name, Katib, means "one who writes." When I told him I was an engineer and drew plans and diagrams, I could see the wheels turning in his brain. He described his own happiness with the house as the completion of a circle that took him from home to faraway places and then back, comparing it with mine, which he referred to as an unerring straight line from one distant place to another. Later on, he proposed that with my interests and abilities I could maintain and preserve the house and even transcribe the writing on the walls, for posterity's sake. That's when he raised the idea of my buying it. I was so desperately keen on Bait Katib that I would have agreed to dance with the devil. He wrote that condition into our agreement, the transcription, I mean, not the dance.

I don't want to give the impression that I was reluctant to do this. I was mesmerized by the beauty of the script and tantalized by the promise of what the words would tell me. Soon after I moved in, I found a scholar to translate them and to teach me the difficult language.

My preoccupation with the house kept the sober reality of the world at bay, but bad news filtered in all the same. George checked up on us almost daily, positive that we'd perished in the previous night's bombings. He took care to prick holes in

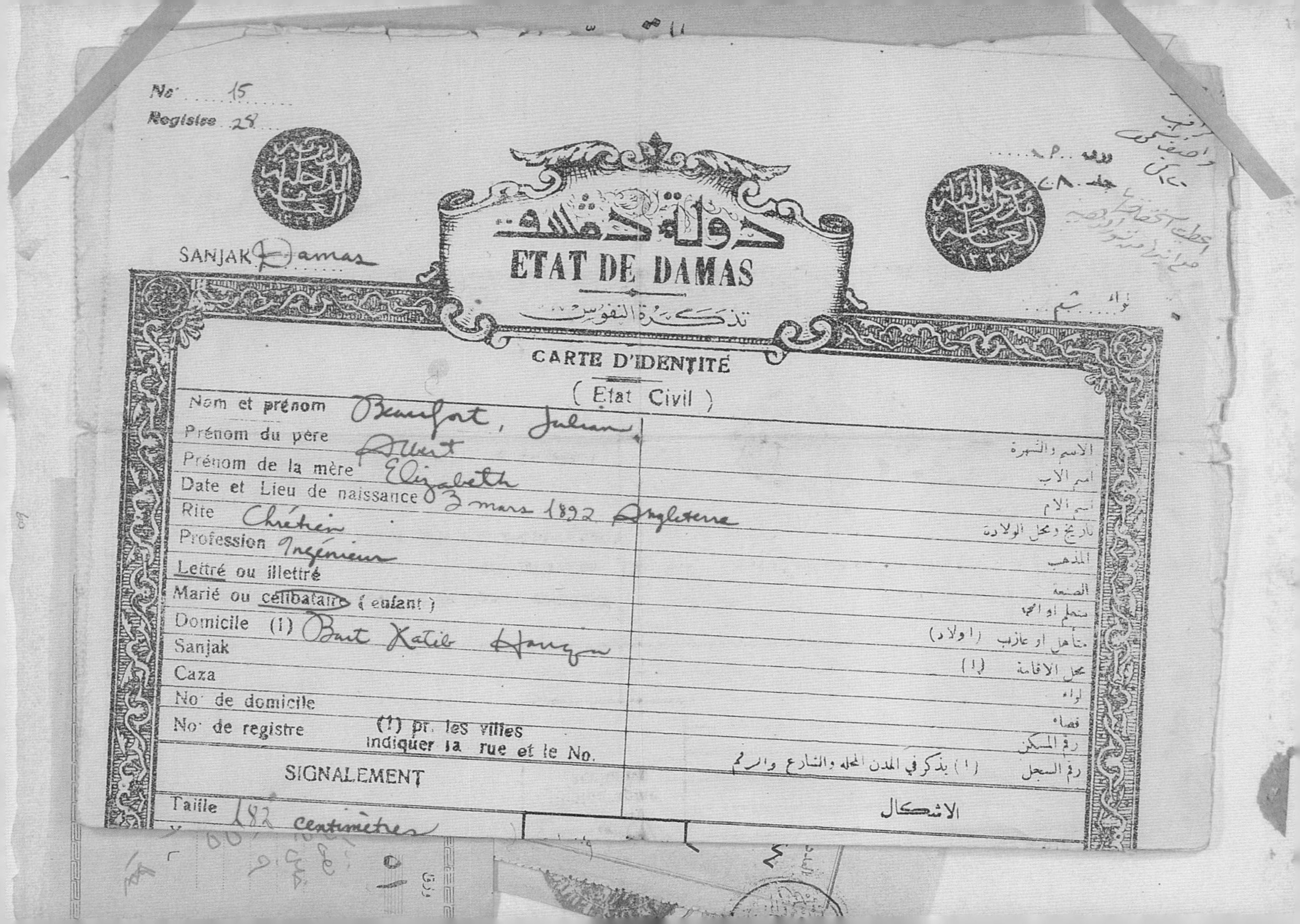

No: 15
Registre 23

SANJAK Damas

دولة دمشق
ETAT DE DAMAS

بطاقة الشخصية (الأحوال المدنية)

CARTE D'IDENTITÉ
(Etat Civil)

Nom et prénom — Beaufort, Julian

Prénom du père — Amet

Prénom de la mère — Elizabeth

Date et Lieu de naissance — 3 mars 1892 Anglais

Rite — Chrétien

Profession — Ingénieur

Lettré ou illettré

Marié ou célibataire (enfant)

Domicile (1) — Bent Kalid Hamyan

Sanjak

Caza

No de domicile

No de registre

SIGNALEMENT

(1) pr les villes
indiquer la rue et le No.

Taille 182 centimètres

ورق ١

my balloon with painful details of new attacks and reinforced barricades.

Foreigners, he thought, were not in any immediate danger, though most French citizens had fled. Of those remaining, many were lying low in the northern suburb of Salhiyya, as it was distant from the heart of the revolt, which was exactly where I was. He pointed out that Damascenes had sheltered many Europeans, but not to be surprised if I encountered resentment. He suggested that I put off sight-seeing and let Najwa and Ahmed deal with necessities until the troubles died down. And he warned me not to wear my hat; the brim was a dead giveaway.

DAMAS (Syrie). - Lieu de Défense devant l'Hôpital Saint-Louis au Kassah.

Ever tried to wear a tarboosh? How do you keep it on? Glue must be involved. Anyway, under the circumstances, getting caught up in a dispute that had nothing to do with me was not high on my list so, for the first few months, I avoided going out. What was happening was too reminiscent of my own war. The lingering, omnipresent odor of burning shot stabbing pains through my head, making me wonder if I'd been patched up all right after all. Whenever I was called upon to show my papers, my wires short-circuited, and I contemplated the pleasure of delivering a sock in the jaw instead.

Unfortunately, cannon fire and aerial bombardment continued long after my arrival. I wrote down somewhere how often that occurred. Let's see. Here it is: November 19th, December 7th, 9th, 11th, 12th, 13th, I needn't go on. When a bomb whistled through the air followed by the silence before the

Sidi
'Amud

Nov. 1925

explosion, time was almost unbearable. Even the house seemed
to freeze and hold its breath. It was better when they fell fast,
their collective din masking that split-second dreadful calm. The
only positive side—from a selfish point of view—was that most
of these attacks took place first in the Bab Tuma quarter to the
east, then in the Maydan to the south.

That I never entertained the idea of leaving was brought
home to me when I had my trunk sent for from Beirut and found
it contained nothing relevant. The clothes were ill fitting; I gave
them away. The medals and the uniform were repugnant—why
on earth had I carted them with me?—I burned them in the
oven. The books seemed to belong to someone else; I donated
them to the consulate library and bought others, more suited to
my new life.

62

There were also some photographs—of a nurse I was sweet on while recuperating. Trouble was, though she was game for a fling, when it came to marriage she preferred a chap who didn't have bits of metal in his brain. I don't blame her; my sole achievement, after two years on the mend, had been the knitting of a scarf. Not to mention that I bored her to tears with all my blather about Damascus, which hardly struck her as a place to make a home. When I tore up her photos, I had nothing left to tie me to the past except a few souvenirs saved from my earlier travels.

My plans to immediately renovate the house had to be postponed. Skilled workmen either were fixing up roads and government buildings or were in hiding, having taken part in the rebellion. Construction materials were in high demand, and there were extreme shortages, mainly because the Syrian livre was tied to the franc, which had taken a beating on the international markets. Taxes and interest rates were punitive as well. Roadblocks and ambushes hindered the transport of stone from the quarries. Even had the roads been open, most trucks were commandeered by the army. Petrol was scarce and extremely expensive. Fortunately, Bait Katib sheltered me from these troublesome realities.

But I haven't described it yet. Not that I can do it justice, not like travelers from the last century—Addison, Porter, Lamartine, Taylor—who wrote so sumptuously of Damascus houses.

Typical of an old city house, its exterior is of nondescript stone, wattle and daub, and wood, with high windows overlooking the streets below. The entrance—the already mentioned large door into which a smaller one is inset—gives way to a narrow corridor that leads, via a right-angle jog, to the courtyard. Before its different wings were sold off—long before my arrival, before I was even born—Bait Katib had four courtyards.

Mine would have been the *haramlik*, reserved, in homes with more than one courtyard, for family and female visitors. Within this courtyard, a large fountain sits directly in front of an open, lofty outdoor room called a *liwan*. *Liwans* are always roofed, with one side open to the elements, and usually face north, that is, are situated on the south side, and my house is no exception.

Starting with the ground floor, on three sides of the courtyard are eight rooms of various sizes. Some have ceilings so high you think that one day you might, like warm air, float up out of reach. Others have such low ceilings that when you step up to the divan the room wraps itself around you and gently forces you down into the cushions.

Directly opposite the *liwan* is the grand reception salon, or winter *qa'a*, so-called because of its southern exposure, while to the east is a smaller room known as the summer *qa'a*. It's cooled by a lovely white marble fountain, shaped like a fluted bowl and fed by a single, central spout.

Along the east side is my study. Next to that, there's a proper *hammam*, that's to say, a Turkish bath. Stone steps leading up to the second floor and down to the cellar—a rudimentary pit for storing vegetables—separate the *hammam* from the kitchen, which is located in the northeast corner. A lavatory, an insalubrious afterthought, is stuck under the stairs. The upper story consists of a covered, cantilevered gallery and nine rooms, two of which are reached only by a set of stairs near the main door. From the main section of the second floor, another flight of stairs climbs to the roof, where there's a pergola and a small shed for laundry and other chores.

The rooftop is where Damascus and Bait Katib really merge. From there I can smell the thick, heady stink of the river or, by turning ninety degrees, the dry, pure desert.

It's at once earth and heaven, where the odor of the rotting straw and hardened mud of the walls and roof mingles with the sublime fragrances that drift up from the barrows of the rose petal sellers, as they make their way to the Suq al-Attarin, the perfumers market.

The west courtyard wall is a two-story façade with false windows and doors only suggestive of rooms. At one time this wall had butted up directly against the neighbor's house, but when I moved in, that building was a pile of rubble, having been destroyed during the fighting; the common wall was the only part standing. I discovered later that this neighbor's house had formerly been part of Bait Katib, so these now purposeless

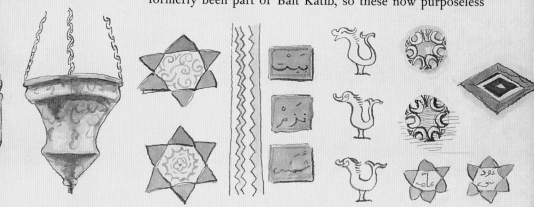

windows and doors had once been functional. For the last half century, however, they had been sealed off with a thick partition of clay bricks.

At the far end of the west wall, the remnant of a corridor—about two feet deep, corresponding to the thickness of the partition—ended with a fake door that not only was nailed shut but lacked hinges as well. If the neighbor's house had survived, the door—assuming it could open—would have led to its courtyard. For the first couple of weeks, in a state of inexplicable disorientation, I tried to leave through this door. If it opened now, it would lead to a public passageway created when the rubble of the destroyed house was cleared.

With some rooms connected to others and some having only one way in and out, the house has the feel of a maze. The deception is compounded by the false west wall and by the repetition of ornamentation throughout that gives the unsettling sensation that one is repeatedly going into a room that is continuously but subtly altered when, in fact, one is moving through different rooms.

Another feature that adds to the sense of displacement is the absence of true angles. The house isn't oriented strictly north/south but is off about fifteen degrees to the west. None of the walls, though, correspond to this axis and, furthermore, none extend in a straight line; they all jog, not only horizontally, but vertically as well. On top of that, one steps up from the floor of the courtyard into each room, but the measure of each step is visibly different. It's as if Bait Katib started out as a single room, then grew—one room at a time—without the benefit of compass, plumb bob, or measuring tape.

Whereas the haphazard alignment gives the house a kind of transience, the ornate décor has quite the opposite effect. Door panels are made with interlaced rectilinear strips of contrasting wood. Their lintels boast complex designs fashioned from different-colored pastes. Walls rise up in alternating horizontal stripes of black, warm brown, and off-white stone. Floors are of multipatterned marble slabs, some in repetitious groupings, others doggedly unique. This ornamentation is overwhelming when taken in all at once, but the eye is meant to look upon details one at a time. I've lost myself to many hours of gazing at a single motif such as a simply painted wreath of flowers. How can artists convey so much about coloring, lighting, shadow, shape, in so few strokes? Geometry also absorbs my attention as

I endeavor to unravel the squares and triangles that so intricately and perfectly circle round each other.

Protecting these features from the rebellion was touch and go. The military frequently demanded entry to search for hidden insurgents or arms, we picked up an appalling number of spent shells off the paving stones, and we were too often ankle deep in soot and ash. We all—Najwa, Ahmed, and I—constantly swept and dusted the charred city from out of our little paradise.

Ahmed and I filled in holes blown out by mortar fire, temporarily propped up the fallen-in roof, replaced the windows, weather-proofed the roof with new straw and mud, and managed to close the main door. But I could never bring myself to repair the damage just outside that door. The bullet marks were a kind of memorial, though I wasn't really clear about it at the time. Now I know why I preserved them. The neighborhood is being so thoroughly rebuilt that there is no memory of 1925 whatsoever, except the change of the quarter's name to *Hariqa*, or fire.

I also looked for signs of Asilah, for it was in these early days
that I developed my need to find out what had happened to her.
Have I mentioned yet that everything in the house had been left
as if she had only stepped out for a minute? In her bedroom, a
mattress lay on the floor. It wasn't stored away in a cupboard, as
is the habit here. Clothes and shoes were scattered about. In the
kitchen, rotting food sat on a table, and dirty dishes filled a bucket.

With so few residents left in the quarter, I quickly established
that no one remaining had any recollection of her after Sunday,
the 18th of October, when the heavy bombardment commenced.
Najwa and I made a list of the neighbors' names and—when we
could find them—their new addresses. I wrote to or visited them
all, and over time contacted almost everyone. It was exhausting
and frustrating but also gratifying, as we discovered many
survivors, including the Majids, who had lived in one of Bait
Katib's former wings. They told me that they had seen Asilah
during the night of the bombing, just as she was leaving the
house. It was the same night that they had lost their son, Selim.

I didn't believe that she had gone to Salhiyya or Beirut, as George suggested. It seemed clear to me, then, that she had been killed. Even so, I had Najwa clean her room and ready it for her return.

Her presence was inexplicably strong, as if she were there with us. At first I dismissed this as sheer nonsense because, in spite of the many rooms, it just wasn't possible for someone to live there undetected. As time passed, however, I wasn't so sure. Now that I'm putting my thoughts to paper, I should pin down what gave me the idea that she was among us.

Well, for a start, her door would be left open, when I know that Najwa always kept it closed. My alarm clock disappeared, and the replacement I bought vanished, too. Books would be left in the oddest places, especially my English/Arabic dictionary, which I would have remembered carrying around myself, because it was so heavy.

This sounds as though I think a poltergeist inhabits the house. How can I express this properly? It wasn't—or rather *isn't,* as the feeling persists—incessant, but when it happens, it's a very strong sensation of being close to a living, but invisible, being. If I'm guessing right, Najwa and Ahmed shared my feeling, but we didn't speak of it for fear that we'd destroy it.

I'm certain it's why Ahmed refused to move out of his tiny room at the entrance. And why Najwa constantly sniffed about like a bulldog rousting out a cat, acting queerest during those times when my own sense of Asilah was most powerful. Take this for example: she regularly cooked for Ahmed and me and waited till we'd finished before she ate. I slipped into the kitchen once when she was by herself. She had set two new places and had dished food onto both plates. While she ate she smiled and pointed to various items, as if urging an invisible guest to sample the olives or the hummus or her wonderful *ataif,* pancakes and cream. When she noticed me standing there with my mouth open, the blood drained from her face, and she ran, crying, from the room. From then on she shut the kitchen door when she ate, but I often overheard her reenacting the same charade.

I may not be driven to share my meals with a spirit, but I do feel I'm being watched. At first, I constantly looked over my shoulder positive that I'd catch someone standing near me. I still hear the muffled padding of slippered feet. Whiffs of sandalwood and amber overpower the roses and jasmines in the garden. These hints of silent movement make me restless, compel me to scour every corner of the house. Night after night—in the torpid heat of summer and the raw, wind-torn winter—I move from one seemingly empty room to the next, preceded by the rustling of curtains. Vases and bowls tremble lightly on their shelves while I stand motionless, but shake when I pass, as though my steps are far heavier than those of the unseen one who I imagine goes before me. Dried leaves and petals already caught in their own vortex pause at my approach, then scatter themselves around my feet and follow me in my relentless pursuit of—of what? A breath, a sigh, a shadow? What propels me into this agitated air for which I can never find substance? Oh, it's easy to blame restlessness, but what do I really think? Do I truly believe Asilah waits for me around a corner, down a hall, on a landing?

I mustn't forget about the fragments of melody, sung from what is at one moment a great distance and then from close by, that tease and disturb me. To drown out these snippets, I hung cages of canaries and finches around the courtyard. When the birds began to accompany the mysterious singer, I went and got a gramophone. The first record I bought was by Oum Kaltsoum. It was then that I discovered that music sent Najwa into rapturous lamentations. Occasionally, I came across her sitting on an upturned pail, listening to the recording, tears

running down her cheeks. Other times, she would dance by herself, a sinuous, rolling dance, completely devoid of sensuality, but disturbing nonetheless. Her very bones abandoned themselves to the minor chords, yet she seemed to control the music rather than the other way round.

Everyone was nuts about the Egyptian singer—her voice was broadcast from every store, café, and home in the city—but Najwa wasn't passionate about her alone. I experimented and bought the recordings of Ajmal al-Ahrani from Aleppo and Nadra al-Shamiyyah from Damascus. Singers of Syrian songs, they had an even worse effect on Najwa than Oum Kaltsoum. Thank goodness, their output was so limited.

By way of explanation, Najwa told me that Muna and Asilah had entertained her for hours when they practiced together, Muna playing her oud and Asilah singing. Hence, her partiality to women musicians. Once I found that out—in the interests of peace—I bought only instrumentals or male singers, like Mohamed Abdelwahab or Shaykh Ahmad al-Shaykh.

Soon after moving in, I bought up a portion of the land to the west, with an idea of restoring Bait Katib's former size, or at least putting some real rooms on the other side of the fake west wall. Worried that the Mandate government could easily refute the deed I had received during the Ottoman rule, I reregistered my ownership. I must get both of them copied.

DAWN

THE GRAMOPHONE CAUGHT JULIAN'S EYE. He carefully dusted off the record that he had left sitting on the turntable, then switched the machine on. The needle hadn't been replaced in years and the record, bought back in 1926, was warped and scratched. After a few seconds of crackling and hissing, Oum Kaltsoum's sultry voice filled the room. He watched the label's spinning blur for a moment, then searched, in vain, for the deeds as the song played. It faded into more crackling. The needle danced over the bumps, producing a low, whooshing noise. Forgetting to turn it off, Julian left the study.

Asilah, who had been listening outside, took advantage of his absence, went in, and placed the arm back at the beginning of the record. This time with her own bittersweet alto joining in.

Footsteps pounded across the courtyard. She fell silent. Seconds later Julian appeared at the door. Tormented by the phantom voice overlying the recording, he ran to the player, swept the arm aside, ripped the record off, and snapped it in two. Then, not believing what he'd done, he stared at the pieces incredulously. With head bowed and shoulders slumped, he slowly walked out of the room.

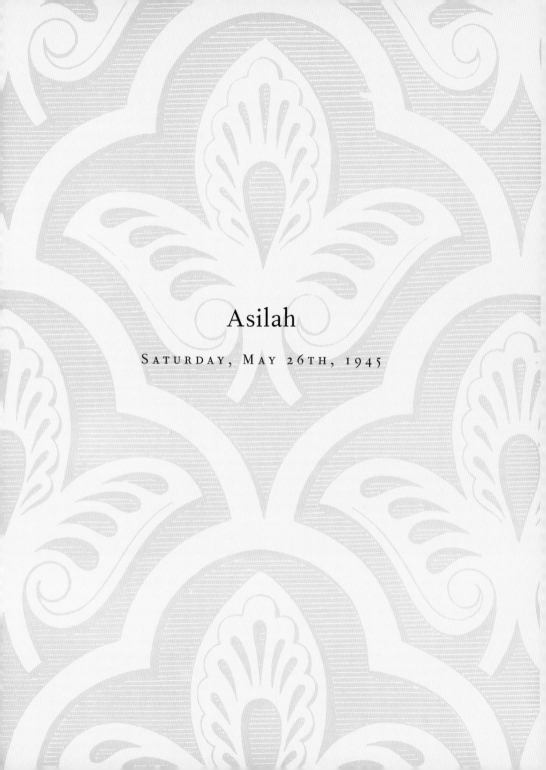

Asilah

SATURDAY, MAY 26TH, 1945

Morning

Asilah knew that she should have resisted the urge to accompany the Egyptian singer, but it had been so long since music had been heard in Bait Katib. It was too quiet, with Ahmed and Najwa gone. Even the birds, which had been replaced over the years, were all dead. She herself had buried the last one a short while ago. Now, only empty cages decorated the courtyard.

She shook off the weight of silence by concentrating on distant street sounds: tinny music, good-natured shouting, interminable car horns. These reminders of life brought her back to the present and the urgency of their situation. Only four days remained before the house was to be lost and, as far as she could tell, Julian had barely taken the necessary steps to save it. It was imperative that he get his papers to the courts. She sighed with relief when she saw his draft letter, but when she read it through, she despaired. It was spineless.

How could she help? She thought for a moment, then laughed out loud. Why am I asking myself this? She shook her head in disbelief. At first I wanted to get rid of him, and then I forgot to think about what I wanted. Now, suddenly, I find myself helping him. Why? Being family, don't my cousin and her husband have a greater right to be here than he? Or have I finally realized how much I need him? That was it, of course, she nodded. She couldn't do without him now; he was her means of keeping the house. But this didn't answer her initial question, of how could she help. She chewed on the handle of the pen.

Of course! She'd write the letter herself! She rapidly listed the arguments she felt were convincing enough to overturn the order. She referred to her father's confidence in Julian's ability to maintain and restore Bait Katib. Swallowing her pride, she called Julian an adopted son and described his valuable work transcribing the history of the wall. She also pointed out—in third person, of course—the likelihood of her imminent return, though actually doing so didn't cross her mind. And she concocted a credible story that Julian had the house only in trust until the family reestablished itself.

Then she dealt with Amin al-Rafiq. She'd never met him, but she knew he was a speculator of the worst sort. Soon after his marriage to her cousin in 1920, he had scandalized the family by buying land under false pretenses, then selling it at huge profit to foreign companies. She didn't have details—and who knew what he'd been up to since—but it would do no harm to allude to his crooked dealings.

Once satisfied, she translated her composition into French, then copied it, painstakingly imitating Julian's writing and his signature.

Julian was fast sleep on the divan in the *liwan*, cradling the fragments of the recording. She slipped the letter under the two pieces of black plastic, letting her hand rest briefly on his shoulder, before working up the courage to run her finger along his brow. He flinched at her touch, his eyes flew open, and he brushed her away with his free hand. Startled, she recoiled. After a second of staring sightlessly, he shut his eyes and slept once again.

The deeds turned out to be in the valise he had carried to the house twenty years earlier. They would have to be copied. Asilah's pulse raced at the idea of taking them to a scribe. She calmed down and tried to banish her fear. She'd need money and suitable clothes. Julian's wallet, which was lying on his bedside table, supplied the cash, the clothing was retrieved from her closets. Finally ready, she went and opened the door.

What she saw left her bewildered. Instead of the narrow, winding lane of her youth, there was a broad street lined with shops, all closed in the midst of the week's busiest shopping day. Had everyone fled? But fled what and to where?

The midmorning light was harsh. She shielded her eyes against it, breathed deeply, and stepped down onto the street. As she inched along, a truck, come from out of nowhere, tore down the road toward her. Its rearview mirror grazed her arm as it sped past. She rubbed the spot, though it didn't hurt in the slightest.

Over the roar of the truck's engine came a loud and haranguing voice, distorted by distance and echo and punctuated by wild cheers. It sounded like a political demonstration, perhaps at the Citadel. The truck squealed to a stop at the end of the street. Just then her hand brushed against the bullet-scarred wall. Her fingers reached out to trace the pitted surface when a white flash—sunlight bouncing off a shop window—seared her eyes, and she panicked and stumbled. She straightened herself up, her heart pounding out of her chest. She remembered the bloodstains that had so frightened her and the unbearable pain that tore across her back on that terrible day in October, which she suddenly seemed to be reliving. The screech of the truck's tires as it turned the corner transformed itself into plunging missiles. The glare from the windows became mute explosions, the roar of the unseen crowd became the drone of airplane engines. Barely subduing her rising nausea, she rushed back to the door and fell into the house.

Humiliated, she made her way over to where Julian slept, pausing to pick a sprig of jasmine from a nearby vine as a comforting token of normalcy, and set the deeds next to the letter she had already tucked under his hand. She sank to her knees and rested her head on the cushions of the divan.

She shook herself, sat up, stuck the jasmine in her hair, and contemplated Julian's immobile but far from peaceful face. There was no doubt that he had aged since he first came to Bait Katib. Already thin, it didn't seem possible that he could have lost more weight, but he had. His clothes fit loosely, as if he were a boy in his father's things. His powerful hands, though, had defied the shrinking of the rest of his body. They were always working, the hands, whether hauling beams or grasping a pen.

Watching him openly like this, she remembered the strain she felt when she still lived like a fugitive in her own house. At some point, however, she found there was no need for such caution, that through a trick of light, or angles, or something, she could get quite close to him without being seen. Yet she knew she disturbed him. The discovery was at once frightening and exhilarating. She recalled leading him on, until one day—. Why daydream this, she admonished herself, when I can write it down. After all, it's a part of Bait Katib's story that Julian does not know. Before she went off to the study, she mischievously shook him awake, then ran away as quickly as she could.

She sat down at the desk and waited a moment before she opened Julian's notebook, listening in case he followed her to the study. Not hearing any footsteps, she turned the pages, captivated by the photographs and drawings with which he filled the margins. What can I do that would even come close? she asked herself. I don't have pictures, and I can't draw. I have only my words, which, I can't deny, look so much nicer than Julian's. But what else do I have? She ran her hand through her hair, retrieved the jasmine, and pasted the blossoms onto the page.

يوم اكتشفت القصر

كان ذاك في لحظة وجدت نفسي في
محنة. كنت قد اختبأت في جورة في
الحائط الذي يؤدي الى الباب الوهمي.
من المؤكد ان جوليان سمعني، حيث انه
قدم باتجاهي مباشرتا. و من خوفي دفعت
بجسدي الى الباب وكنت قد نسيت انها
مغلقة بالمسامير. لكن كانت مفاجأتي
انها تدا عت.
وخرجت من الدار، ليس الى باب الجيران ان
كما كنت انتظر، او الى الزقاق، بل وجدت
نفسي في ساحة كبيرة تحيطها اعمدة في
ثلاثة اطراف. وتدفق الماء مرحبا من نافورة
ملاقة و مرط الساحة. وغطت حيطا نها
شجيرات الورد وزهر العسل و الياسمين
الجونفيلا ولفت غصو نها الاعمدة
حيطة باطراف الساحة. وكان مفاجأة لي
انني تجمدت في مكاني. وتداركت الى
مسامعي خطوات جوليان التي بدت انها
تقترب من خلفي. ومن دون ان انظر
الى الوراء، هرولت الى لحوش و منه الى

و غطت خلال رواق المتعددة الذي ...
والبرتقال زوايا الساحة الاربعة.

The day I discovered the palace

It was one of those moments
when I was nearly cornered. I
had hidden in the recess leading to
the false door. Julian must have heard
me for he headed directly toward me.
Alarmed, I pushed against the door, forgetting
that it had been nailed shut. To my amazement it gave way.

I stepped out, not, as I had expected, into my neighbor's
house—or rather, the lane it had become—but into a large courtyard, colonnaded on three sides. Water bubbled welcomingly
from the immense fountain in its center. Fig, lemon, and orange
trees shaded the four corners of the space. Roses, honeysuckle,
jasmine, and bougainvillea climbed the walls and twined around
the pillars. In my surprise, I had paused. Julian's steps were close
behind. Without looking back, I ran into the arcade and from
there, up a set of steps, to the nearest room. Still, he approached.

There was no other apparent exit; if he came in, he would
see me. My only choice was to hide, but where? There were
three platforms in the room, each a step up from the *'ataba*, or
lower central floor. I leaped onto the platform on my left and
rushed toward a cupboard set into the wall, intending to crawl
in. But before I could reach it, Julian entered. He made a quick
circuit, his eyes troubled and searching though apparently obliv-
ious to both me and his surroundings. He then walked out.

Why couldn't he see me? I collapsed onto the divan and
shook my head, amazed. Am I a jinn? I pinched my wrist until it
hurt. No. A spirit doesn't feel pain, doesn't need to open doors
in order to pass through them and—I stood up and looked down
at the depression where I'd been sitting—doesn't leave dents in
cushions. Had I somehow stepped into another world? How
fabulous, I thought, if this were so.

Turning back to consider the room, I couldn't help but think it was the finest *qa'a* I had ever seen. My feet sank into silk carpets, the patterns of which echoed the painted walls. My hands stroked brocade shot through with gold. Shafts of light playing off the threads led my eye to the bay windows behind each platform. Each was enclosed by a latticework screen and had ledges wide enough to sit on.

I looked up from the windows to the elaborately painted, lofty ceiling. Instead of flaunting the typical repetitious designs that mimic a carpet or a field of flowers, each beam and plank was painted with dwellings and temples, wild landscapes and gardens, and earthly and heavenly skies. The effect put me in mind of storytellers who unravel their tales over many nights or of an enthralling ride through the streets of a magical city. At the junction of the ceiling and the walls was a many-tiered, honeycomb-like *muqarna* border interspersed with panels inscribed with lines of poetry, done by a calligrapher whose hand rivaled my father's.

Cupboards—such as the one I had first thought of hiding in—were built into the walls. Each was enclosed by doors inlaid with mother-of-pearl. I opened up the one nearest to me. It would have been a tight fit! On its shelves were Turkish ceramics: ewers, cups, and rosewater sprinklers, glazed with tulips, roses, carnations. There was glassware as well: decanters and bowls, gilded and incised with floral and geometric patterns. The other cupboards held similarly beautiful objects. One had an array of silverware, another, embroidered textiles.

I crawled over to the window and peered through the screen. All that I could see of Damascus had been reconstructed, and it was beautiful beyond words. The dome of the Sinaniyya Mosque reflected gold and lapis lazuli; minarets everywhere glowed. Orchards lapped up to the city walls like green waves upon a shore.

The vista was a living interpretation of the ceiling. I could imagine the artist sitting in this very spot, inspired by all he saw.

I poked my head out to look at the passersby. The clothing the women wore! Veils of carmine or turquoise or amber were draped over robes of contrasting hues, creating a street awash with the palate of a watercolorist gone ecstatically mad. On their feet these multicolored ladies wore dizzyingly high *qabaqib* inlaid with colored stones and mother-of-pearl. At the sight of these wooden clogs, I squinted and rubbed my eyes. They were no longer worn—outside the baths, that is—and none so elaborate were seen these days.

Men riding horses and donkeys eased their way down the narrow lane. Their turbans were fanciful creations: candy stripes, starry skies, sunbursts. A troupe of camels crossed the junction at the end of the street. Their bridles and saddle blankets were fitted out in scarlet, indigo, ivory, and orange. Why, my street had been repopulated with a crowd of veritable peacocks!

Where was I? In Damascus to be sure, but where in Damascus? The house clearly belonged to someone, but whom? I couldn't be just next door to my own Bait Katib; there were no neighboring houses anymore, not since the rebellion. Unless this house was built quickly, without my even noticing. And if I wasn't next door to Bait Katib, where was I? Suddenly worried about being caught trespassing, I hopped down from the platform and onto the iridescent cobalt blue and aqua tile of the *'ataba*. Passing its small, ornate fountain, I hurried out into the now-empty courtyard.

Without pausing to speculate further, I ran to the door and stepped across the threshold, back into Bait Katib. Shutting the door behind me, I could think of nothing but the splendid house. Its magic may been due to its grandeur and exquisiteness, but the scenes I had viewed from the window were too incredible to be real. To prove to myself that I'd been dreaming, I went up to the roof. As I expected, around me lay a wasted, ravaged Damascus.

I tried to reopen the door, but it was sealed shut, as it had always been. At that moment, I believed that my discovery had only been a fantasy. As I now try to recapture why I had accepted unquestioningly what I had just seen, I can't help but let what happened after color my thoughts.

AFTERNOON

A DOOR SLAMMED. Asilah hastily shut the book and wiped off the pen. She went out into the courtyard. The *liwan* was empty; Julian must have gone out. She collapsed onto the divan and was lulled to sleep by the still-warm cushions.

Julian

SATURDAY, MAY 26TH, 1945

Late morning

Blasted fly. Julian brushed his cheek. A second later, he slapped at his nose, then drifted off into an uneasy sleep. He woke up with a start, dreaming that someone was shaking him. "I slept too long," he muttered. As he shifted his weight, papers crinkled underneath him and something snapped. From under his hip, he yanked out the papers and the now-smaller and more numerous fragments of the broken record.

Among the papers was a bizarre letter that he must have composed sometime during the night. Not only could he not remember writing it, but the grammar, the vocabulary, the style, everything, was all wrong. Had he been that upset? He scrutinized the penmanship, laboriously shaped as though he'd been trying to remember his own handwriting. Then he reread it. He hadn't ever thought about being an "adopted son." Moreover, he didn't know any of these details about Amin al-Rafiq, and though it had already occurred to him that he could use Asilah's possible reappearance as an argument, he hadn't worked it out so clearly. The idea that he had the house in trust was terrific, but not his. And where had the deeds come from? He shook his head, rubbed his eyes, then went to dress for the law courts.

Still pondering the origin of the letter, he walked through the city streets. Shuttered stores reminded him that yet another general strike had ground the city to a halt. Until the strike was over it was useless looking for a scribe to copy out his deeds. He stood in front of the courthouse, trying to decide his next move. The place usually swarmed with lawyers, plaintiffs, defendants;

now only a few men hovered. He asked one of them if he had any idea when the building would reopen. The man woefully shook his head and showed him a briefcase crammed full of papers.

The entrance of a nearby office building, obscured by the engraved brass plates of *avocats*, *importateurs*, and *agences comptables*, caught Julian's eye. Betting that lawyers discreetly ignored strikes they themselves didn't provoke, he climbed the stairs, ready to take a chance on anyone with a law degree. The two on the second floor were absent. He climbed to the third floor and tried more doors. All locked. On the fourth floor, a Karim al-Halabi agreed to give the papers a once-over.

In his late thirties, Halabi wore a red rose boutonnière, which he sniffed frequently. The office was surfeited with a mélange of fragrances from roses standing in vases and dried rose petals filling bowls. To Julian's appreciative remarks, Halabi said, "The rose, like the Barada River, is one of the great pleasures of Damascus. According to tradition, that is," he added, with all the caution of an attorney. He chose an especially perfect blossom, clipped its stem, and stuck it in Julian's lapel. "There," he said, admiring the effect. "Now you are truly a man of Damascus."

Scent and heat rushed to Julian's head, making everything at once very far away and too close. He held onto the desk for a moment to steady himself. Then with exaggerated care he unfolded the crumpled, smeared papers and handed them to Halabi, who raised his eyes but said nothing.

The lawyer studied them and Julian's own documents carefully. "I'll help you," he said finally. "But don't expect anything more than a delay, at least in the short term." He sat back. "You see, there are several solid arguments against you. First. You aren't Syrian. Second. You aren't a Katib." He smiled. "Or are you?"

Julian shook his head. It was hopeless. Why had he thought otherwise?

"On the other hand," Halabi continued, "there are several points in your favor. You've occupied the house for twenty years, you were never notified that this action was in process, and the transfer period is too short." He paused and scribbled a few words. "Furthermore, as you have already specified, Asilah Katib's death is not established, so there's a chance she could eventually reclaim the house. Best of all, Rafiq is likely unaware of the revised deed issued during the Mandate and of the purchase of the additional parcel of land." Halabi waved the Ottoman document in the air. "How wonderful that you have this," he said. "They destroyed so many records when they left. Almost no one saved their own copies.

"As for the proposal that you could be called the caretaker until Asilah Katib's return, there's no better reason for getting rid of you; many Damascenes would covet such a job." He clicked his tongue when he read the accusations against Rafiq. "A last resort," he advised.

Halabi set the letter aside. He now spoke quickly, having warmed up to the task. "You see these affidavits?" he pointed to the papers clipped to Rafiq's document. Julian nodded. "These people—religious leaders, tax collectors, so-called neighbors—support Rafiq's claim of ownership. You need to counter with testimony from your own neighbors, friends, servants."

"Najwa and Ahmed, who worked with me, they're both dead. So is Burhan Efendi, my Arabic teacher."

"I'm very sorry. And George Samad, the original notary?"

"He moved to Canada. I'll try to contact him."

"Your neighbors? You have tenants, perhaps? Shopkeepers?"

"I had no neighbors for the first, almost ten years. It took Hariqa a long time to reestablish itself, as you know. And the shopkeepers are on strike. I don't have a clue how to get hold of them." As he talked, Julian realized he'd been slowly cutting himself off, burying himself deeper within the house.

"Get whomever you can," said Halabi. "We must act as soon as the strike ends. The Mandate is crumbling fast, and transactions carried out during its years could easily be overturned by a new government. I'll drop by Bait Katib as soon as I have anything to report. Don't worry. If we can achieve nothing for now, neither can they."

Grateful to have someone to leave the papers with, Julian walked back to the house, but he couldn't shake the dizzy feeling that had come over him while sitting in Halabi's office. He was overwhelmed with the difficulties, despite the lawyer's plan of action. Why didn't he just tell Rafiq and his wife that they could have the house when he died? He was over fifty and had no heirs. So maybe they'd have to wait twenty, thirty years. Was that such a long time?

Should he propose this to Halabi? He stood outside his door for a moment, undecided, absently sniffing the rose. The heavy fragrance evaporated his hesitations. He made his way to the study, set the flower down on the desk, and took up his journal again.

رقم القطعة N° de la Parcelle	رقم الصحيفة N° du Feuillet				دولة سورية ETAT DE SYRIE			المكتب العقاري Bureau Foncier	
۲۰۹۲ حرف B	۲				سند تمليك ***TITRE DE PROPRIETE***				مكتب

المنطقة العقارية
CIRCONSCRIPTION FONCIÈRE — القسم
Section

Nom de l'Immeuble ـــــــــ اسم العقار بيت كعب

Condition juridique ـــــــــ نوع القضائي ملك

Nature du droit ـــــــــ نوع الحق ملك

الشارع والرقم
Rue et Numéro — المحل المعروف
Lieu-Dit

حريقة

No du registre — الخارطة PLAN — رقم السجل

Description de l'immeuble وصف العقار

LIMITES الحدود — CONSISTANCE DE L'IMMEUBLE

AT DE SYRIE
DIRECTION GÉNÉRALE
ES SERVICES FONCIERS
ET DES DOMAINES
Conservation Foncière

دولة سورية
المديرية العامة لمصالح العقارية
واملاك الدولة
المكتب العقاري في لواء شــ

۸۰۸۲

(سند التمليك)

TITRE DE PROPRIÉTÉ

Circoncription Foncière ـــــــــ المنطقة العقارية

Parcelle N° ـــــــــ قطعة رقم ۲۰۸۲ حرف B

Titulaires du Titre				اصحاب السند
ملحوظات OBSERVATIONS	محل الاقامة Domicile	تاريخ ومحل الولادة Date et lieu de naissance		اسم صاحب السند وتابعيته ومهنته Nom, Prénom, Nationalité et Profession du titulaire du titre
	بيت كعب حريقة شم	الكترا، ۱۸۹۲		جوليان بيروت

۱۹۳۷ آب ۱۱

الترقيم	قيود السجل اليومي Référence au reg. Journal	Inscriptions	التسجيل	السجل اليومي Référence au Reg.
	Date ... No ...	Motif ...		

PERFICIE — MOUKATAA — IDJARATEIN		الأول الفقرة ٢ — حق السطحية، المقاطعة، الاجارتين		لتسجيل

adiations	الترقيم		Inscriptions			اليومي
الاسباب	السجل اليومي Référence au	Cons.	الاسباب		اسماء والقاب واصحاب الحق	Ordre Référe

Deuxième Section du

حقوق التأمين (بيع الريع — البيع بالوفاء — التأمين) قصر حق الت

CHRESE - VENTE A REMERE - HYPOTHEQUES) RESTRICTIONS AU DROIT DE DIS

OBILIÈRES — ACTIONS — RESTRICTIONS

DE DISPOSER

— الفقرة — ٢ الحجز العقاري — الدعاوي — قيود حق التصرف

ESSAROUF. WAKF. USUFRUIT.				الأول — الفقرة — ١ — الملكية ، التصرف ، الوقف ، حق الانتفاع		التسجيل

diations	الترقيم			Inscriptions			التسجيل
الاسباب Motifs	قيود السجل اليومي Référence au Reg. Journal Date التاريخ | No الرقم	توقيع امين السجل Sign. du Cons.	الاسباب Motifs	الحصص Parts	اسماء الملاكين والمتولين واصحاب حق الانتفاع Noms des Proprietaires. Moutewallis et bénéfici	اليومي Référer Reg. Jo

العشاء
EVENING

1926–1927

The new year began with more bombings and an increase in
military force. It was a cold, dreary, wet winter, filled with
suffering and privation. The homeless—and there were many—
warmed themselves by burning the few trees left in public
gardens, stripping the city of its greenery, and infusing the air
with the scent of eucalyptus. I can't imagine how many trees in
courtyards such as mine were sacrificed in private. Not that
there were many courtyards left. It's estimated that Hariqa alone
lost three hundred houses.

Until the following summer, tanks rolled up and down
Straight Street, and machine gunners patrolled the narrow lanes.
I didn't get out much, but I was constantly worried for Najwa
and Ahmed, who roamed fearlessly in search of news, food, and
fuel. Their reports disturbed me but sharpened my interest in
what was happening. They found out when rebels had been
captured and whose door was plastered with posters demanding
the occupant surrender or face arrest or execution. With so
many of the political figures hiding, exiled, or imprisoned, it
was no wonder that people were terrified. Even so, there was a
very low rate of compliance to the demand that insurgents and
arms be turned in, as sympathy for the revolt was growing
stronger, even after many months of privation.

The Maydan quarter where Najwa lived became the target of
reprisals, and Omar Bey, one of its leading citizens, was assassi-
nated. I begged her and her family to move in with me, but her
husband—a sickly sort with a chronic and understandable distrust
of foreigners—categorically refused. To make matters worse,

Mitrail

Les tranchées dans les jardins

her son Shukri had joined the rebels, and she went for weeks at a time without hearing word of him. In April, the fighting there was so intense it was a miracle that anyone survived, yet the worst was yet to come. In the first week of May, as many as a thousand homes and shops were destroyed or damaged by firebombs. The death toll was extremely high, no matter whose statistics you believed.

TYPICAL OF THE FRENCH FORCES IN DAMASCUS: AN OFFICER WITH HIS DETACHMENT OF COLONIAL TROOPS IN CHARGE OF A MACHINE-GUN POST AT A STREET BARRICADE.

Nov 15th 1925   Illus. Ldn News

Miles of barbed wire surrounded us, but it wasn't clear what it was supposed to hold in, let alone keep out. It was as if this prickly cloak that our city wore was the only way the military could think of to shackle our hands and feet, so to speak. They weren't successful. In the *medina*, where rooftops were as important thoroughfares as streets, people easily avoided the barriers. Bait Katib, now isolated from its neighbors, wasn't part of anyone's path, but from its roof I watched young men scrambling on all fours and dropping out of sight down some stairwell, shrouded women loftily trespassing across their neighbors' terraces, and old men pelting the Senegalese soldiers below with rotten fruit or potsherds.

Damascus had a tenuous hold on sanitation at the best of times. Now it got really nasty. Trash clung to the barbed wire. The lanes, which were normally muddy only when it rained, became a constant mire of soot and the sewage spewing from broken pipes. The sentries used any surface to piss on and, as for latrines, they hadn't even the decency to squat out of full view.

Packs of hungry, howling dogs roamed at night, often ending up as quarry for bored soldiers. Come morning their carcasses littered the paths. By the afternoon, these motley hunks of piebald hair and flesh would be trampled on or kicked aside. Those hounds that survived cowered in dark corners, pathetically nosing through piles of rotting garbage and otherwise occupying themselves by scratching equally famished fleas from their mangy hides or hoarding the remains of newborn kittens, for nothing—not even war—stopped Damascus's cats from dropping litters faster even than the rats.

By the end of summer, the hardships had lessened and a kind of calm had been restored. People returned and salvaged what little they could of their homes. But when the rubble was carted away, it wasn't clear where the streets, never mind the houses, had been, especially in hard-hit quarters like mine. Discussions got under way about what to do with the bits worth saving. In Hariqa, it was all razed in the end, except for Bait Katib, the Bimaristan Nur ad-Din, Bait Mardam Bey, and a couple of other buildings on the periphery.

I got out more, especially visiting houses in areas that had been spared. At first I was haphazard in my approach, stopping at places I found on random walks, many of which I had already seen in 1914. I became more systematic but had a devil of a time getting hold of a map that gave street names or identified even public buildings. I finally found a pretty good one done in 1924 by two German fellows. It had been in the archives of the French Institute, which operated out of the 'Azm family's former palace.

I've forgotten to mention that the 'Azms' palace had been burned and sacked in 1925 by rebels who believed that the High Commissioner, General Sarrail, was in residence at the time. He wasn't, but they set the building

[B] = Bait
K = Khan
☪ = mosque / jāmi
(H) = Hammam
(m) = mausolée / Turba
C = Café
Y = Cimetière

Photographie Bonfils, successeur A. Guiragossian
157 DAMAS. — Intérieur d'un Bain Turc.

Suq an Saraja

al-Manahiliyya   al-Malik
                 az-Zāhir

Saqqa
Amin

ar-
Naufara

Quwatli

Derwiche Quwatli   Katib Madam   Rue Droite   'Azm
Basha   Bey

Sidi
'Amud

Sinan   Malas Zainab 'Ayta   Saurvaf
Basha   Sibā'i Daskun

                    Ahmad al Sayid   Quwatli
                    Karlas   Tiba   Ali Aga
                       Towfiq   Hulwan
                        'Allui   Araqsasi

                                                  Bab
                                                  as-

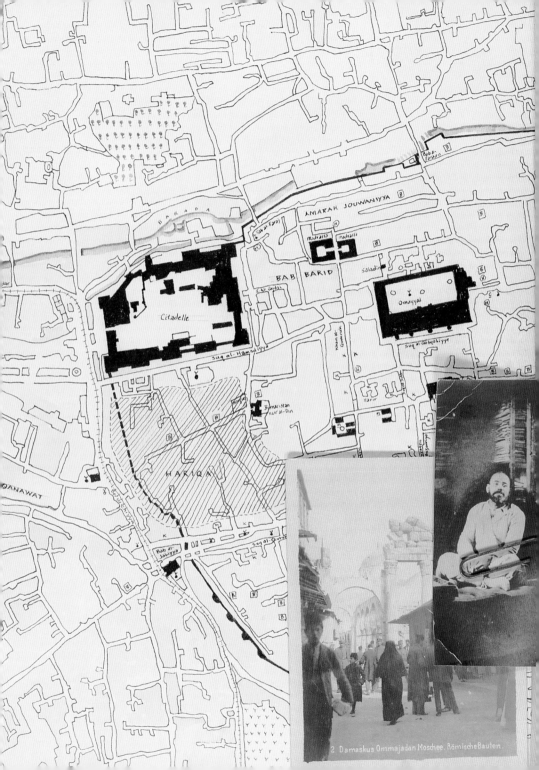

BARADA

ÁMARAH JOUWANIYYA

Madrassa   Madrassa

Saladin

BAB BARID

S. al Qirdi.   Omayyad

Citadelle

Sūq al-Gabgābiyye

Suq al-Hamadiyya

Khan el Gumruk

Harir

Bimaristan
Nur al-Din

HARIQA

QANAWAT

Bab al-
Jabiyya

Suq al-Q...

2. Damaskus Ommajaden Moschee. Römische Bauten.

and archives on fire anyway. They also stole or busted up museum pieces and ruined photographs and negatives. The luxurious *haramlik* suffered the most structural damage.

That reminds me of Alice, a Parisian I met at the 'Azm palace ruins—tiny thing, she should have been at home, cowering under a bed. Instead she was out, cold-shouldering sentries, upsetting officials by disregarding warnings, taking pictures, and painting. She took me around and got me into houses that I would have never found on my own. I showed her Bait Katib, but she'd not been there for more than a quarter hour—she'd gone to freshen up—when she came out, as pale as a ghost, insisted on leaving, and wouldn't explain what was wrong. We saw less of each other after that. She moved to Salhiyya, then left altogether in the summer of '26.

The map, however. During my wanderings, I diligently filled in its missing street names. For streets without signs, I'd ask bystanders at the beginning of that street what its name was, then ask again at the other end and, more often than not, get a completely different answer. I should also say, these weren't really streets, more alleys, even corridors. Many were cul-de-sacs, but you were never sure till a closed door at the end blocked your way. A dead end could fool you by taking a sharp turn, becoming a clear way through.

I marked down *suqs*, public fountains, cafés, shops, tombs, mosques, baths, schools, and khans, but paid special attention to the houses, examining their construction, looking for ideas. My explorations also put me in the way of some pretty good salvaging, and much of Bait Katib's improvements owe plenty to houses too damaged to restore.

I'd sketch everything that caught my eye, and I'd buy photographs of houses from Fareed al-Kaylani, the photographer who used to be on boulevard de la Victoire. Some nights I'd have splendid lantern slide shows in the courtyard. Projecting

these miraculous pictures of beautiful houses onto the walls of my own beautiful house produced layers of richness that made me giddy. My audience was almost only ever Najwa, Ahmed, and sometimes George, and none of us ever tired of the spectacle. With canaries chirping, music playing, and Najwa making sure we had plenty of lemonade and sweets, I wanted those evenings to last forever.

I couldn't limit myself to simple rebuilding. My head spun with the most fanciful notions. I'd dream up extravagant houses filled with opulent furnishing and adornments. It always happened in the same way: I'd be restless, disturbed. Perhaps a bird had flown in through an open door, or a voice from outside had penetrated the thick walls. I'd walk around the house, up the stairs, through rooms, out to the street. Then I'd find myself back at my desk, pencil in hand, not sure how I got there, not really sure if I'd even left. At my fingertips would be drawings of these splendid palaces, creations that I'd evidently conceived of myself. How this is possible, I cannot say, for I haven't the capacity to imagine such things.

The first sketch I made was of a sumptuous salon—something out of an Ottoman palace like the Topkapi in Constantinople— consisting of three spacious platforms, each backed by a large bay window. Covering these windows were *mashrabiyya* screens, overlapping slats of fine-grained wood. Cupboards set into the walls had doors inlaid with mother-of-pearl. I drew details of these then, as if I had opened each one and peered inside, sketched their contents, all kinds of pots, platters, and jars. Over several days, I drew out plans and elevations and drafted cross sections, showing an elegant vaulted ceiling.

I sketched a gorgeous *hammam* with a many-domed ceiling into which holes had been punched and inset with thick purple and green glass, as well as a tiny, perfect courtyard with one wall taken up completely by its fountain. I transcribed, in passable Arabic and

Ottoman Turkish, fragments of poems I'd never read or hadn't been aware of reading. Although these texts weren't perfectly rendered, I would have been proud of them all the same, if only I could have remembered doing them myself!

I kept coming back to that first room, adding to it until there was space for nothing else, then I'd start over, redoing and refining it.

My preoccupations didn't stop me from trying to trace Asilah's whereabouts. But with an estimated death toll of ten thousand between 1925 and 1926, finding her was hopeless. I've already written about searching out her former neighbors. I also thought of checking with her in-laws who'd moved to Beirut, where I caught up with them in the fall of '26. They'd lost contact with her after she'd moved back with her mother and were embarrassed not to have asked her to come with them.

cedre

3.5'

3'

Ottoman
furniture

10"

20"

20"

Iznik
"Damascus"

4"

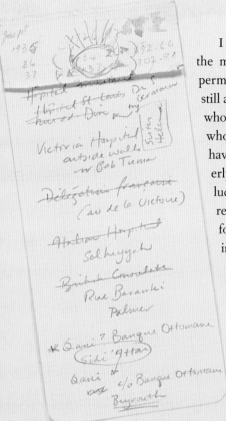

I met with the police and the military, scoured the meager hospital and prison records I was permitted to see, tracked down school friends. I still ask everyone I meet, everywhere I go. Those who knew her grab my arm in sympathy, those who didn't usually ask to see a photograph. I have none, and I can't even describe her properly. I feel as foolish not being able to give a lucid description as I feel trying to explain my relationship to her. I've never found the right formula and generally escape by tapering off into an incomprehensible babble.

My vague recollection of her has become obscured by features of other young Damascene women. I look for her in every woman I meet or pass in the street. I only realize how hard I stare when veils that have been loosely tossed over the hair are pulled tight across faces as I near.

I did have a photograph, briefly, found in a box of Muna's keepsakes. I had thought Asilah's hair long, black, wavy, though I had never seen it out of the knot she wore it in. It was, in truth, shoulder length, brown, straight, and full. Her nose had seemed to me broad and flat, as did her face, but her photo showed a narrow, straight nose and a face that was round and well proportioned with a strong chin. She was relaxed as she looked at the camera, and though she wasn't smiling, highlights in her eyes betrayed good humor. Her large, dark eyes had been about the only thing I had remembered properly.

She wore a dark dress that came to mid-calf, revealing thick, glossy stockings of the sort still fashionable here. Her brimmed hat was finished off with a veil that hung down her back. On her feet were patent leather shoes. The studio set was faintly visible in the background.

Missing were all those things that photographs don't show. Like the quality of her skin. I picture it as rich and tanned, or perhaps I'm fooled by my memory of the warm August light. And the photograph hid her shyness. Or was she shy? Perhaps I'm mistaken about the reticence that was apparent whenever we met. I remember that she was hospitable at first, though in a vaguely obligatory way, as if I didn't register. Then, after I bought the house, I didn't see her at all before leaving. I hate to think that I made her ill at ease.

I can't recall her speaking voice nor if the few words we exchanged were French or English. When we shook hands was her hand warm or cold? What did she smell of? Roses? Amber? Did

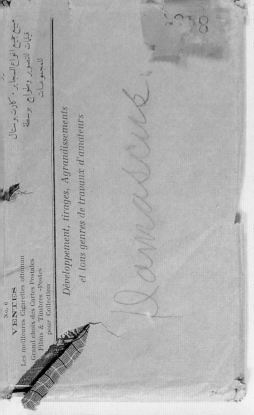

her dress rustle like watered silk? If I could have held her, how would she have felt in my arms? Oh bother. How easily I'm distracted. It's a measure of my solitude.

If I'd thought about it for even two seconds, I'd have hidden the photograph away but, in a moment of sheer idiocy, I showed it to Najwa, who immediately begged me for it. I promised to make her a copy, but when I got ready to go over to Fareed's studio the next day, I couldn't find it. She'd swiped it and cut out the face to put in a locket. When I accused her of theft—not something lightly done here—she willingly confessed. "I want to fill my eyes with her face," was her excuse. But so did I.

I can go for months without a thought of her, then suddenly—perhaps while gazing at the stars or preparing some wood for a new coat of paint—something will brush against my arm or breathe down my neck. I often hear faint murmuring, and my spine tingled when I accidentally discovered that this sound had a word for it, *zajal*, a low hum made by jinns at night. I'm sure it's her. Capturing the sensation is as impossible as tethering a flock of swallows.

I became even more certain that Asilah was living among us during the ongoing translation and restoration of Nasim's inscriptions on the courtyard walls. As I worked it seemed as though every word I wrote down was being checked and measured by an invisible critic. When I made an error, and this happened frequently, I felt jolted by some kind of chimerical disapproval. When things went well, my spirits would race along as fast as my pencil, cheered on by an enthusiasm that can only be described as something "in the air."

Fortunately, my Arabic teacher, Burhan Efendi, with his linguistic feet on the ground, kept me sane. Or sort of sane. He came once a week—Tuesdays, always—to help with the translation. A pious man, he had a face as lopsided as a clumsy self-portrait. The asymmetry was odd and unsettling in this city of perfectly fashioned features. If I sat on his left, I saw a different man from when I sat on his right, yet both profiles were handsome and complete. Looking him straight in the eye gave me vertigo.

As I got to know him better, I learned that his piety was not ironclad. He liked his wine—possibly more than the next person—and would have been mortified to discover that his habit was common knowledge, even though he confided in everyone, including me. He also desperately wanted a second wife—and was fully in his rights to take one—but he was too stingy, and so squandered his precious allowance of forgivable sin on prostitutes. Once I understood the schism in his heart between heaven and earth, his two faces made sense.

Burhan Efendi was an excellent teacher but prone to ambiguity. He advised me to learn Arabic by forgetting English, saying that when I'd mastered Arabic, I could relearn English. Baiting him, I asked if he could tell me how I had learned French concurrently with English. He rather doubted that, he replied, then tricked me into agreeing that I must have forgotten one in order to acquire the other. When I asked if I had to erase both from my memory in order to learn Arabic, he solemnly cautioned me not to disappear under the weight of trying to forget.

As Burhan Efendi's time was limited, many were the days when I worked on the translation with Ahmed. A slow and unsteady reader, Ahmed helped to the best of his abilities. Because he refused to learn any French or English, it's more thanks to him than my teacher that I'm fluent in Arabic.

Ahmed's mind was a wonderland of possibilities enhanced by his love of hashish. I doubt if he had ever entertained the idea that there might be only one answer to any question. Or anything less than a hundred thousand shades of gray. Even the setting of the sun in the west was a subject for discussion. To a question such as, "What exactly does *tala'a* mean?" he'd discourse for an hour. "One might say," he'd begin, then I'd learn how this simple word meant much more than to rise. With it one appeared, erupted, sprouted, got into a train or a car, read, studied, looked, shone, informed, became acquainted, asked someone their opinion, and so on, and so on.

No one would guess he carried around so much knowledge, frail as he was. Still in the rags he was wearing when we first met, it seemed as though anything he knew would have trickled out through the rips and holes long ago. I gave him money for new clothes, but he gave it to his deceased wife's sister. Then I asked Najwa to go shopping with him, and *she* came back reoutfitted. It was hopeless, he simply didn't want anything, though he did have a newish turban reserved for Fridays. After wearing it to the mosque, he washed it out and hung it from the line on the roof. A weekly ritual that was never missed.

Erroneously expecting that he'd soon want to move into the house proper, I set up his Spartan cell at the entrance only temporarily. No larger than a storeroom, with an ill-fitting door and a single, wooden-shuttered window, it caught and held the freezing winds of winter and consumed the hot air of summer. He refused any luxuries save a kapok-filled quilt for the dead, cold month of *kanun at-tani*, and he grudgingly allowed the installation of a threshold sill to keep out rainwater. I added a mosquito screen one summer after seeing his face splotched with bites.

Partly because of his reticence and partly because of my own uncertainty, I had the nagging suspicion that Ahmed disapproved of my owning Bait Katib. But when I finally asked him if he considered me an intruder, he looked surprised. "You belong here," he told me. "You give the shadows life." As I write this down, I wonder if I've been looking for Asilah in all the wrong places.

If I had asked Najwa her opinion, I know her answer would have been straightforward and harsh. We got along fine as long as we kept to safe topics. In fact, she taught me Damascene Arabic, an argot that even today is confined to the city.

Her mental *daftar an-niswan*—or book of women's knowledge—was a wealth of detail. I'll never know why she shared it with me, unless she saw in me something other than male. I've often heard Englishwomen proudly declare that they are treated as honorary men in Arab society. I can't think why I should be pleased to be regarded as an honorary woman. Nothing I did—drinking alcohol and not wearing a veil excluded—conformed to Najwa's masculine ideal. From the first day, she never covered her face in my company, nor hesitated to speak of the most intimate details of her neighbors' and friends' lives. I knew who was pregnant before their husbands knew, and who'd had their virginity salvaged (virginity here being a reparable physical condition, not a state of mind, like back home).

Najwa showered me with cures for both impotence and too much vigor. When I pointed out that my single state so far negated the need for such stuff, she concocted love potions. I pretended to take them and regaled her with stories of the women who couldn't keep their hands off me. She so clearly didn't believe me that I wondered what these potions were really supposed to do. When my hair started thinning, I declined her offer of some foul-smelling restorer. Unfortunately, my hair had never grown back properly at the base of my skull. She clucked about the mess of scar tissue and, during the hot months when the skin became irritated, treated me with cooling balms.

It's not surprising that between their three languages—Najwa's of society, Ahmed's of subtleties and complexities, and Burhan Efendi's of scholarship and sin—I have become immersed in a dialect of which little that is said leads directly to its true meaning. Immersion, in my case, has not led to faultless understanding. Though I've mastered the forms, thanks to a good memory, I am sorely unable to unravel even the most transparent of paradoxes. Much of what bewilders me can likely be attributed to the weaving of God in and out of every sentence, since God and I long ago parted ways in a fog of mustard gas. That this evident flaw was overlooked by my three teachers was a tribute to their indulgence.

I'm forgetting the walls. When it wasn't Burhan Efendi's day and when Ahmed was otherwise occupied, I'd work on them by myself. Reading much like Genesis with a fair share of "begats," the wall's history begins slowly and repetitiously, but soon becomes a spirited account of the Damascus social scene as it revolved around many generations of the Katibs. On one line we read serious commentary: fiscal reform, for example, and on the next line, gossip: the birth of an illegitimate son of a *qadi*, in one instance. Because successive heads of the family were official scribes to the Ottomans, they were privy to the affairs of sultans and governors. I seriously doubt that Nasim missed chronicling a single one of the many intrigues swirling around their courts, including their plots to rid themselves of Napoleon—whose nickname, *as-Sultan al-Kabir*, the Big Sultan, was as pathetic as it was amusing.

The massacre of 1860 has a place, complete with the names of those who had taken shelter in Bait Katib during the worst of the ravages and descriptions of Nasim's courageous relatives and friends. Ahmed was ecstatic when he found that not only was his father 'Abd al-Ahmed at-Tawil mentioned but that he was deemed a hero, along with the famous, exiled Algerian rebel leader 'Abd al-Qadir al-Jaza'iri. Originally from Morocco, Tawil had come to Damascus in 1852 with 'Abd al-Qadir and married a Damascus girl shortly after. Ahmed was born sometime before the riot, the first son of nine, and the only one to survive into the twentieth century. We amused ourselves in speculating that baby Ahmed might have been brought to Bait Katib for safety during the riot and marveled at the fate that led him back here.

With regard to the house, I learned that Bait Katib, at its height of prosperity, had consisted of four main sections, each with its own courtyard, the *haramlik* for the family, the *salamlik* for general receptions, a *khadamlik* for servants, and a fourth for a school for calligraphers, which I can't resist calling a *calligramlik*. The size of the household—family, servants, and students—can only be imagined.

Built into the exterior south wall, as is the case today, were shallow kiosks for shopkeepers to operate out of. Elsewhere were stables, which were sold off in the mid-nineteenth century, as was the *salamlik*. I don't know what happened to the former, but the latter became the neighbor's house, which was then destroyed in 1925. The wing housing the calligraphy school was sold in the 1890s when Nasim cut back on teaching. It, too, was destroyed in 1925.

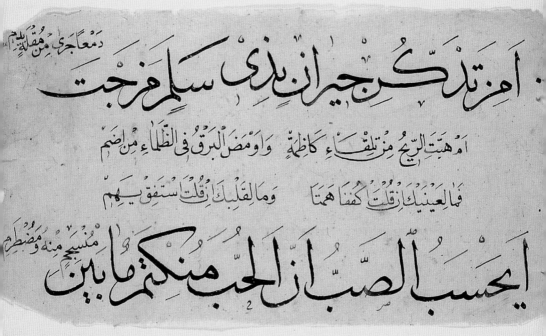

Interspersed with history are tips on the art of writing, as though Nasim planned his lessons during breaks in his chronicle. Included are instructions on how to seamlessly join sheets of paper and how to age them with fig juice and saffron or prepare them for calligraphy with alum and egg white. There are tips on how to extend gold leaf, so as not to appear miserly.

Spacing of letters and use of ornamentation augment suggestions for correct hand movement, rhythm, and breathing. Nasim also detailed his schooling in Arabic literature in Beirut and in the scribe's arts in Istanbul from the venerated teacher, Kadiasker Mustafa Izzet Efendi.

None of this, however, excited me as much as my discovery that Nasim had written me into the history of Bait Katib. There I was knocking on his door, along with our mutual delight in shared interests, my fervor—that's the word he used—for Bait Katib. He had written that he knew he was about to die and was worried for the future of the house, and that he had sold it to me, because he trusted me to cherish not only the building but its past as well. And he wrote that I had promised to finish the wall.

I'm not satisfied with my fulfillment of that promise, but I don't know what else I can do. Relying on Najwa's memory, I composed a broadly sketched history that spanned from Nasim's death until the rebellion in 1925. Then with Burhan Efendi's help, I refined the Arabic. I worked hard to capture Nasim's style, and when I got as close as I'll ever get, I had the wall replastered, traced the words onto the new surface, and had the relief work done.

Then, as Nasim wished, I copied everything onto big sheets of thick cotton stuff known here as *qutni*. Only a month ago, I bound them and the translations into a portfolio, which I took to the museum for safekeeping.

I still don't understand how the story of Bait Katib should be completed, nor how I can do it when I don't know the fate of the last member of the family. The unknown conclusion is not going to write itself. One way or another, I have to find out what happened.

قلم كسمك و طوقنتق اصولى

قلمى اولاشن يازمق ابوكومى مقدار تحفه اشاغيدكى وجهله طونغرى

Ottoman ع

NIGHT

JULIAN SAT BACK, pushed his notebook around for a minute, then lit a cigarette, only to stub it out after a puff or two. It was hot that night. Beads of sweat dripped down his forehead, dampness stained the armpits of his shirt. A sudden gust swept across the desk, though the curtains did not move.

He looked to the window and stretched out his hand to locate the source of the breeze. It caressed his cheek and drew him into the courtyard. He followed it as he had so many nights before.

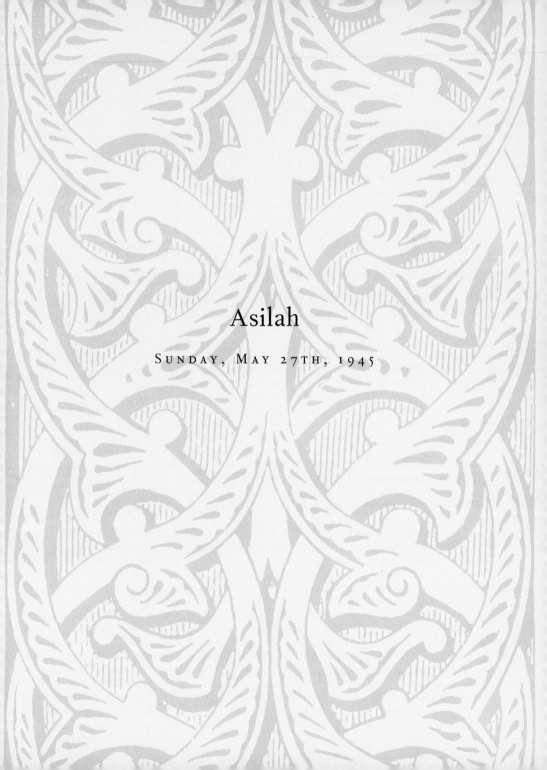

Asilah

DAWN

ASILAH CIRCLED ROUND HER OLD ROOM, breathing deeply as though inhaling something of her former life, then drifted back out and along the gallery, leaving the door ajar. An early desert wind howled through, whipping up tapestries and rattling windows. She could feel her sense of existence evaporating; she was somehow slipping away. But as she fought to restore a sharp image of herself, the wind swept her mind clear.

Returning to the study, she shut out the gusts and ran her fingers over Julian's notebook, now more than half full, bulging with scraps of paper and bloated with watercolor. She flipped back to the entry for May 26th. He had written nothing to indicate what he'd done to get the appeal launched. And, as far as she could tell, he hadn't brought back the deeds or Rafiq's document. Was he so foolish as to leave the originals with the court clerks? She cursorily searched the room, but there wasn't even a receipt for the papers. Back at the desk, she randomly turned the notebook's pages.

She read of his Arabic lessons and of Burhan Efendi's advice to forget in order to learn. I've forgotten so much, she mused. In order to learn, what? My memories are like—she stroked the darkened petals of the rose lying on the desk, then crushed them between both hands and held them to her nose, breathing in the powerful scent her warmth had recaptured. They awakened in her fleeting pictures of gardens and laughter. That was it—she picked up her thread of thought, as she scattered the petals across the pages of the journal—my memories are like this flower. No matter what fades, there's still a vestige that can be roused.

She longed to share her language with Julian. But what could she give him that Najwa, Burhan, and Ahmed could not? She pondered the question to no avail, then turned to another page where she found his description of Bait Katib's former grandeur.

She'd already learned, by reading the wall as she sat with Julian while he worked, that Bait Katib had been immense with several wings all serving different functions. With each new room or wing revealed on the wall, she reclaimed another room, another wing in her palace, as though the words were giving back what was hers all along. Yet it wasn't until she had finally overlain the descriptions of this long-ago Bait Katib with mental images of her palace, that the connection between the two had become clear; the wall described her palace.

Julian was inadvertently opening up for her a past that would have otherwise been lost. His special love for the house must have been why her father had chosen to give it to him, though she couldn't imagine that her father would have foreseen the fantastic results. And, she mused, picking up her pen, I still don't understand why I now have this palace and what, if anything, it has to do with Julian, except that without him it wouldn't exist.

وفي يوم من الايام
سنحت لي الفرصة
ان اطر منه
المساعدة.

قصري ينمو

وبالرغم من ان عقلي كان يعرف انه ليس
هناك خارج الحجرة الحمراء، لكن قلبي اقتنع ان
هناك بيت غريب وخرافي. وحاولت عدة
مرات ان افتح الباب ولم استطع، واصبحت
على قناعة اني بحاجة ماسة الى جوليان.
كنت اراقبه من خلال شباك مكتبته و
وقف فجأة وتقدم نحوي. ووصل الى
المكان المقصود، لكنه توقف من دون حراك.

ومسكت انفاسي، وزحف برص على الرصيف الحجري، ورفرف
الحمام باجنحته، ومن بعيد تداعت اصوات
ابواق السيارات الرتيبة.

وفجأة اغلقت النافذة وبعد وهلة قصيرة استدرحته من
وافزعته بلطف. خلال نفس الباب، والتي انفتحت
بسهولة مرتا اخرى الى ساحة التكشفتها
حديثا. لقد اصابتني الهلوسه. انني بالفعل
حية! وبعد ان مررت من خلال القاعة
الجميلة، وجدت نفسي في ممر
طويل على كل من جانبية ستة اطواق
تؤدي الى حجرات. وتصاعدت
خطوات جوليان من خلفي.
وقل يهمهم من نفسه: "ان كان

My palace grows

Although my rational mind knew that nothing but a passageway lay beyond the sealed door, my heart believed in the strange and fabulous house. I had tried to reopen the door several times without success and became convinced that Julian was somehow essential for me to unlock it again. One day, I saw my chance to enlist his help. I was watching him through the window of his study when he suddenly turned and stared straight at me. He came to the threshold and stood motionless, attentive.

I held my breath. A gecko scrabbled along the paving stones, pigeons under the eaves fluttered their wings, from off in the distance muffled car horns harmonized.

Then I slammed the window and startled him quite nicely. I soon lured him through the same door—which once again opened effortlessly—and into the newly discovered courtyard. I was delirious. It did exist! Passing the beautiful *qaʿa,* I found myself in a long hall with six archways on either side, each leading to a room. Julian's steps echoed behind me.

"Well," he muttered, "whoever it was is probably far away by now. Still, it's worth a look." He peered through each archway. He didn't see me, even though I walked with him.

After he left, I explored. In one bedroom, I found a proper bed, not a mattress to be rolled up and stored away in the morning. A closet was filled with my clothes, a cupboard contained my personal mementos, a set of shelves held my books. Deeply thrilled, I couldn't help but claim this room, indeed the whole house, as my own. How fantastic, I thought, Julian has helped me build a new home, and I don't have to share it with him. In my excitement, I forgot that I needed him to get in, and more important, that I wanted to be with him.

The growing house is so magical and astonishing that even now I'm not sure I've found it all. I seem to stumble upon more rooms each time Julian follows me, though I'm careful not to lead him on too often; after all, it takes time to appreciate the rooms that I've already discovered.

There's a salon with walls covered in mosaics fashioned from thousands of tiny pieces of beveled mirror that transforms the viewer of the wall into ornamentation. Dozens of luxuriously furnished bedrooms have their own distinct décor, their own incredible vistas. I can sleep in a different chamber every night and wake up in a new world every morning, fresh with dreams filled with people and events well beyond the scope of my knowledge and understanding.

Rivaling the most splendid *hammam* is a cavernous hall with large and small pools and a many-domed ceiling, inset with colored glass to admit the sun. The constant, melodic flow of water; the steamy, ethereal atmosphere; the subtle waves of perfume; and the soothing, conquering warmth give me such pleasure that I almost hurt from the fear that it will be taken away from me.

Another immense hall is divided into three distinct sections: a library, packed with books and manuscripts; a scriptorium, overflowing with parchment and papers, pens, and inks; and a printing workshop, with three presses and cabinets of Roman, Arabic, Hebrew, and Greek type. Light pours in through large, well-placed skylights and windows; low tables and chairs are

ويبد و ان البيت
يزداد نموا خياليا
الى درجة انني
لا اعرف ان كنت
قد اكتشفت كل
ارجائه. ويبد وا
انني اعشر على
حجر جديدة كلما
يتعقبني جو
لكنني حريصة
ان لا استدرجه
مرات كثيره ، حيث
انني احتاج الى وقت
طويل لتأ قلم واتعود
على كل حجرة
اكتشفها حديثا.

يـل جدا.

جوليان

في بناء

هذا المنزل، لكني غير

مجبرة لان اشاركه

فية. وانستني فرحتي

انني بحاجة الى

جوليان كي ادخل

البيت،

والاهم من ذلك

انني اريد ان

اكون معه.

arranged to best catch that light. Doors open up to a shady loggia through which one enters a small and private courtyard. I remember discovering this hall; I had read my father's description only the day before. It was so accurate and complete that I became confused and believed I had been pulled into a fable.

Rooms continue to transform themselves with each visit, growing in size or becoming more sumptuous. It's as if I'm seeing—in the space of days and weeks—their evolution over many years, perhaps even centuries. Yet, other aspects are almost normal: day becomes night, the seasons pass; flowers and trees in the courtyards blossom, bear fruit, shed their petals and leaves, and then start all over again.

The contrast between the starkly, simply furnished rooms of the old place and the opulent salons of the new is startling. I have few reasons to go back now, but when Najwa was still alive, I liked to be near her, and she often left me a plate of something delicious to eat. Many times I was tempted to let her know I was still alive. But I kept having second thoughts. I continued to worry that I would lose my home; then when I stumbled across the palace, I became doubly worried, as I had so much more to lose. Once I became confident that my new home couldn't be taken away from me, I feared that I would frighten her too much. Most of all, though, I had become accustomed to my new life and cherished my ability to drift in and out of company at will.

But even though Najwa is gone, I still go back, irresistibly drawn to Julian, to be his shadow. I miss him when I'm in the new palace; it's incomplete without him, just as the old Bait Katib is incomplete without me. There was a time I even worried that he might leave. Was it then that I realized I had to do whatever I could to make him stay and be as happy as possible? That's why I helped him with the translation and with his drawings.

Then I fretted that he would marry and bring his new wife into Bait Katib, a thought that vexed me as I had no right to be jealous. I admit I tried to make him fall in love with me. I filled the place with perfumes and put out a photograph of myself—one that I actually liked—in the hopes that he'd find it and think about me. I didn't count on Najwa taking it! I also chased away a couple of women whom he brought to Bait Katib. Silly things. I'd said no more than "Boo," to them, and they were gone.

I often catch Julian prowling around my exquisite palace, as if he's not only restless but as if he senses something special beyond what he sees. Once, he relaxed on one side of my fountain while I sat opposite. Where did he think he was? I splashed water on him, not out of malice, for I thought he would not feel it, but out of sheer amusement. He stood up straight away and looked at the sky, which was pure and blue—not a cloud in sight—and wiped his face with his handkerchief, saying, "Funny. I wonder where the water came from." He walked away, still looking around, as I laughed.

How could it have taken so long for me to see that my palace was Bait Katib? Oh, not the one of today, but the one of long ago, before it was impoverished by time and circumstance. When Julian sketches the rooms that he doesn't know he's seeing, he's re-creating Bait Katib of the past.

So, by bringing him here, I am giving him something, after all.

وبعد أن ترك المكان،
استكشفت المكان
لوحدي. ووجدت
سريرا مناسبا وليس
فراشا من النوع الذي
يلفلف ويُخزن في
الصباح. وكانت هناك
خزانة مليئة بملابسي،
وخزانة اخرى مليئة
بذكرياتي الخاصة،
ومجموعة من الارفف
عليها كتبي. ومن سروري
رغبتي العنيدة في السيطرة على
أن هذه الدار هي غر
أن الدار كلما

Morning

ALTHOUGH ASILAH HAD LONG ACCEPTED that the palace was the past, she had never before reasoned it out so clearly. Now that she had put her thoughts into words, would she be allowed in without Julian's help? She set down her pen, carefully closed the book so as not to crease the rose petals, and walked out of the study. She crossed the courtyard and pushed against the door. It was still firmly closed.

Julian

SUNDAY, MAY 27TH, 1945

Nº 142. Maison Ali Agha, Damas. F. Kaylani

Morning

WHAT A PERFECT MORNING, thought Julian. The sun's heat was temperate, and a light breeze from the west carried with it a crisp smell of the Lebanon Mountains. He was up on the roof, lying on his stomach and watching the deserted street, hoping Halabi would appear. A book lay open under his hand, but he couldn't concentrate on it for longer than a few minutes at a time. He looked at his watch. It was eleven o'clock. Shouldn't I be doing something? he asked himself. Then he remembered. He was supposed to be tracking down witnesses to his ownership of Bait Katib so, after listing possible names, he took off to see whom he could find.

All of the streets around his house were absolutely empty, the shops were closed, and there weren't the usual children around who might lead him to the owners' homes. He strolled over to the telephone office with the idea of trying to locate George through the long-distance operator. But the building was locked up tight. Then, because he was nearby and because the strike hadn't affected the foreign bookstores, he spent the rest of the morning, first at the Foyer and then at the Universelle, searching through the few available books dealing with property law. They all tidily skirted his situation.

In the end, buying nothing except a copy of Ambler's *Coffin for Dimitrios*, he headed back into the old city to the Bakri baths near Bab Tuma, taking a chance they were open. After steaming the last three days out of his pores, he went to Halah's coffeehouse south of Straight Street. Here again, he was in luck. It was open for a few hours that afternoon. Like Bait Katib, the café had been one of the few buildings hit during the bombardment that had managed to survive. Consisting of layers—a portion of one wall had been part of a stable, another was made up with blocks of Roman stone—it was no wonder it had grown back out of the destruction, timeless and only superficially scathed. He had hoped to get Halah to attest that he had been a neighbor and a customer for the past twenty years. Unfortunately, the café owner was absent, and a new helper was there in his place.

He tucked himself in a corner, rudely turning his back to the other patrons so as not to get drawn into discussions about the strike. Conversations here were always in the form of debates and, no matter what his opinion, because of his foreignness, he was considered a perfect opposition. Alternately drawing long, intoxicating drafts of perfumed tobacco smoke from a narghile and sipping hot, cardamom-scented coffee, he frittered away the afternoon following Dimitrios's tracks as far as Bucharest. After catching himself nodding off, he forced himself to get out and walk.

He wandered down to Bab as-Saghir, the Little Gate, which led to the cemetery where Ahmed was buried. It was too late to visit the grave, so he stood at the padlocked entrance and made do with a touch to his forehead and chest.

Back at Bab as-Saghir, he was suddenly very hungry. He bought some fresh bread—the bakers always managed to stay open during strikes—and munched it as he made his way back to the house. The familiar and simple taste of the warm, unleavened loaves heartened him, quickening his resolve to finish the journal.

LATE AFTERNOON

1927–1935

Can I single out an event during this time to which I can affix a date? I don't think so. Too much that happened was as water in a stream, flowing without interruption or definition.

The political machinations largely passed me by, in spite of my efforts to keep track of them. Arab newspapers, like *'Alif Ba* and *al-Ayyam*, did little to iron out the complications of the nationalist movement, the birth of the National Bloc party, and the day-to-day status of the Mandate. *Le Réveil* and *La Syrie* were no better, and such English papers as I could get my hands on were more concerned with Palestine. Elections, demonstrations, and strikes had virtually no relevance to my life.

The rest of the world was even more remote, except for the panic of '29, which put a dent in my income, crimping my day-to-day living, and forcing me to postpone any major work on the house. To get through I took on odd jobs: translations for George, a balcony renovation for one of his friends, and letter writing for people Najwa dug up.

I even drove tourists and freight to Palmyra and Baghdad for the Nairn brothers' transport company, generally taking two to three weeks to complete a run.

Eucalyptus Euphrates
Deir ez-Zor

132 MUAHALLA AT SUG-AL-SAFAFIR

ELDORADO PHOTO
BAGHDAD

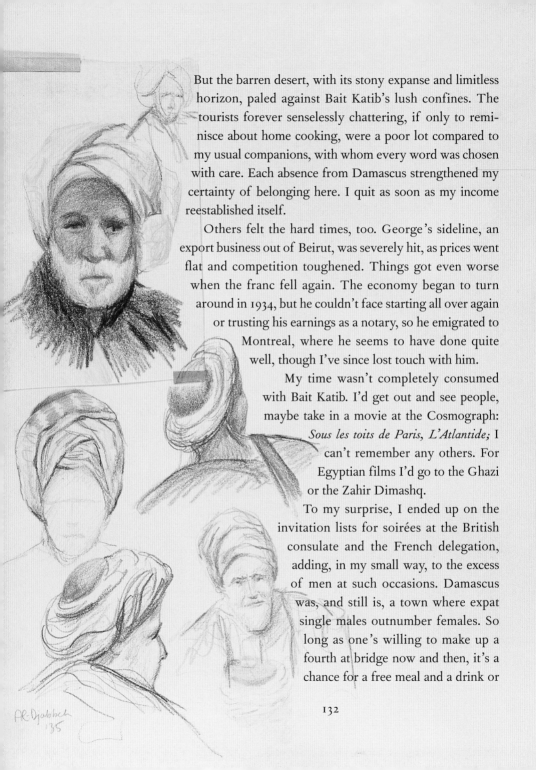

But the barren desert, with its stony expanse and limitless horizon, paled against Bait Katib's lush confines. The tourists forever senselessly chattering, if only to reminisce about home cooking, were a poor lot compared to my usual companions, with whom every word was chosen with care. Each absence from Damascus strengthened my certainty of belonging here. I quit as soon as my income reestablished itself.

Others felt the hard times, too. George's sideline, an export business out of Beirut, was severely hit, as prices went flat and competition toughened. Things got even worse when the franc fell again. The economy began to turn around in 1934, but he couldn't face starting all over again or trusting his earnings as a notary, so he emigrated to Montreal, where he seems to have done quite well, though I've since lost touch with him.

My time wasn't completely consumed with Bait Katib. I'd get out and see people, maybe take in a movie at the Cosmograph: *Sous les toits de Paris, L'Atlantide;* I can't remember any others. For Egyptian films I'd go to the Ghazi or the Zahir Dimashq.

To my surprise, I ended up on the invitation lists for soirées at the British consulate and the French delegation, adding, in my small way, to the excess of men at such occasions. Damascus was, and still is, a town where expat single males outnumber females. So long as one's willing to make up a fourth at bridge now and then, it's a chance for a free meal and a drink or two, but nothing more. I don't go as often now as I used to. The questions about why I'm hiding away in Damascus tire me. People think I'm a recluse because of the war. Let them. They'd never understand my real motivation.

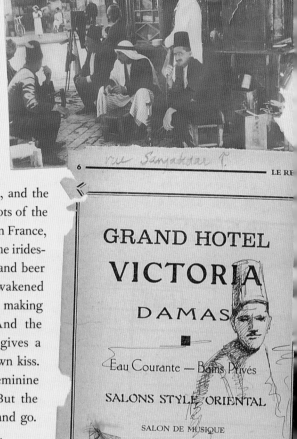

But anyway, better places for a drink are the Olympia, the Splendid, and the Pavillon Bleu. In the twenties, as depots of the absinthe that could no longer be sold in France, their tables were nightly dotted with the iridescent green stuff. Now that whiskey and beer have taken over, the drunks have awakened from their wormwood-fueled stupors, making these dance palaces far livelier. And the mandatory swing round the floor gives a chance for a nuzzle, if not a full-blown kiss. At the very least, I can count on feminine companionship, however fleeting. But the women there, and men, too, come and go. Few have made Damascus their home.

The cafés—especially those along the river, like the Al-Jabbeh—suit me better. Give me a cup of thick, black Turkish coffee and a narghile, and I'll sketch away entire afternoons. Evenings are squandered listening to musicians or storytellers. For people watching though, I prefer the Sanjakdar Street cafés, the haunts of the young politicos: Paris-educated lawyers and agitators, who wear fezzes and read the Cairo papers. Along this street, dubbed "rue Sainte Jeanne d'Arc" by French soldiers, there's a constant parade of pedestrians, trams, buggies, Chevrolet cars, and Renault *camions*.

La maison de l'agitateur Nessib-el-Bakri, détruite à la dynamite.

Le mouvement antifrançais de Damas a eu pour principal instigateur un certain Nessib-el-Bakri, dont la propagande contre nous a commencé dès le début de l'insurrection druze. Lors de la répression des troubles, sa maison a été occupée et, comme châtiment, détruite à la dynamite.

D'une façon plus gnérale, la situation d'ensemble en Syrie et dans le Liban ne laisse pas que d'être sérieuse. Les foyers de rébellion se multiplient un peu partout et ont une tendance nettement accusée à s'étendre vers le Nord. Depuis la fin de septembre, des groupes de « brigands », qui sont en réalité des rebelles, se livrent à des attentats presque quotidiens contre la voie ferrée et sur la grande route de Beyrouth à Damas et, plus récemment, contre la voie ferrée

Through my house-crawling habit, I met Fakhri al-Barudi, who owns a fantastic place in nearby Qanawat. I've spent countless hours there, sketching and photographing. [Note to myself: Ask Barudi to attest to my owning Bait Katib.]

Barudi was one of many prominent men who had fled or been exiled in the twenties. Others included Fawzi ibn Isma'il al-Ghazzi, Jamil Mardam, and Nazih Mu'ayyad al-'Azm. I visited all their houses. Ghazzi, poor sot, was poisoned by his wife in 1929. Mardam became the PM in '37. He'd be a significant witness, if I can reach him. And there must be an 'Azm who would help me.

I also visited the enormous homes of the Jaza'iris, the 'Ajlanis, and the 'Abds (who owned the Victoria Hotel), not to mention houses in the Christian quarter, the Jewish quarter, everywhere. Closer to home, the Quwatlis, Kabbanis, and Bakris regaled me with descriptions—no doubt enriched by the passage of time—of the houses they lost in 1925.

I'm trying to pin down exactly when the rebuilding of Hariqa began. Looking through my old guidebooks, I'm reminded that the 1933 *Guide bleu* map shows the quarter as a blank spot, as does the 1934 *Cook's*. No labels, no explanations. Were the maps warning tourists that they'd fall into a void if they ventured off the colored sections? Would a more recent guide tell me that I continue to live in a *medina incognita*?

I took an Englishwoman around in the spring of '28, and recall her horror at the state the quarter was in—called it a slum—so it must have still been a mess. I think the word escaped

Bait Stanbouli – qa'a
liwan

Bait Shamiyye –
haramlik

Bait Ali 'Agu – qa'a

Rue droite nr Bab ash-Sharq   Bab al-Jabiya

out of shock, as she was otherwise quite a sport. A couple of
years older than me, affable but not at all pretty, she was on her
way to being fluent in Arabic. She had come to stay in Damascus
for a month or so. I offered to put her up, but she found Hariqa
too depressing. An afternoon spent at Bait Katib with the chaos
of rebuilding was enough for her. She took a room in an
appalling apartment crammed to the rafters with crying babies
and ended up falling quite ill. Someone later told me she'd
moved to Baghdad, of all places. A most unusual woman, but
for the life of me, I can't remember her name. The Syrians were
absolutely captivated by her. Ahmed called her an empty book,
meaning that her pages were still to be written, and urged me to
marry her. Ahmed, for whom life was usually so complex, had a
very simple view of relations between men and women. For me,
I wouldn't have contemplated such a step, even if she would
have had me; it would have been a betrayal, somehow.

In any case, by the thirties my neighborhood had settled into
a semblance of normalcy, though it was nothing like it had been
before the revolt. Then, as now, vacant lots dominated, but
otherwise it was jammed with shops, tenements, five- and six-
story office buildings, and right-angle streets plugged with
smoke-spewing vehicles, making it more like a squalid European
town than a quarter in old Damascus. However, the Barada
continued to feed my fountains, vendors declaimed the mythical

qualities of their oranges or almonds or melons, and the muezzins cried out their calls to prayer from newly rebuilt mosques.

My renovations continued apace. Ahmed saw to that, hiring and firing laborers, supervising the laying of new mosaics, inspecting materials, and negotiating costs. *"Ma'laishes,"* *"yallahs,"* and *"'aiwas"* constantly echoed round the place. I pitched in on the actual labor if it involved something that I couldn't mess up, like hauling planks or mixing mortar; otherwise, my role was to draw up plans and pay.

Repairing marble paving stones, we found the remnants of a narrow trench that had traversed the courtyard. This mystified me until I read the section of the wall recounting how houses were equipped with streams upon which trays of food floated from one courtyard to another in order to save steps and preserve the modesty of the harem. We traced the trench to the west, blind wall and could see—with a bit of scraping at the stucco—the outlines of a horseshoe-shaped hole that had been filled in. This confirmed that Bait Katib had extended farther to the west.

Zebdani '34

Bludan 30?

Aleppo '34

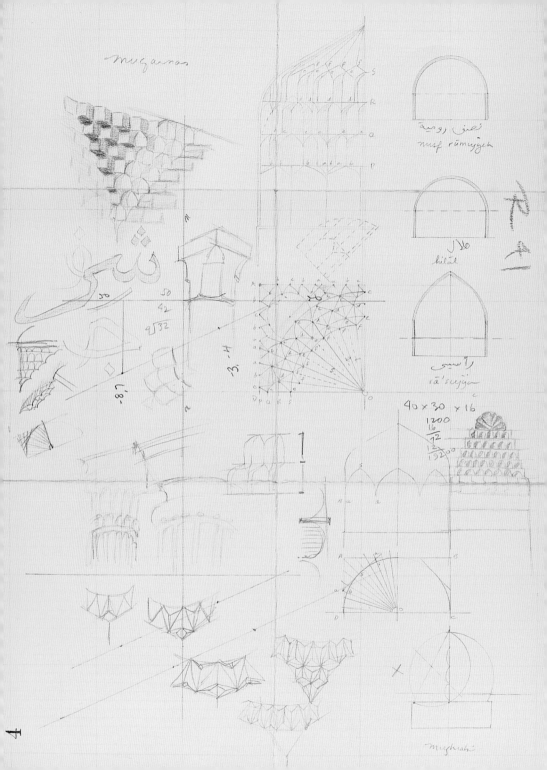

muqarnas

مصف وسی
nisf rūmiyyeh

هلال
hilāl

رأس سجة
rā'siyya

50
42
9√32

3·H

40 × 30 × 16
1200
16
72
½
192·00

muqrabi̇

4

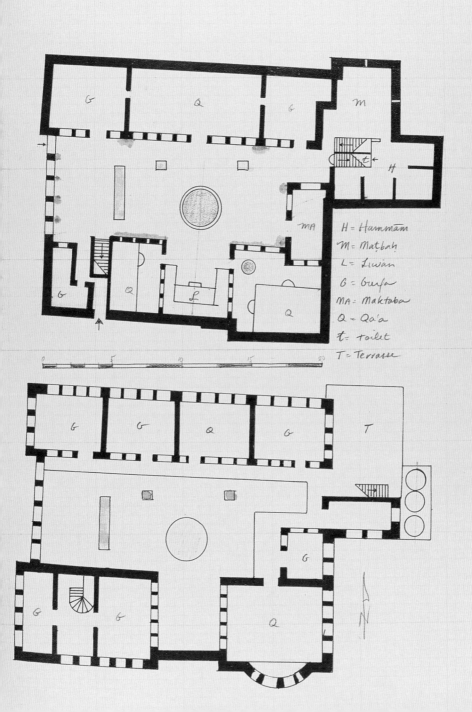

H = Hammam
M = Matbah
L = Liwan
G = Gurfa
MA = Maktaba
Q = Qa'a
t = toilet
T = Terrasse

G   Q   G   M   t   H   MA

0   5   10   15   20

G   Q   G   L   Q

G   G   Q   G   T   G   Q   G

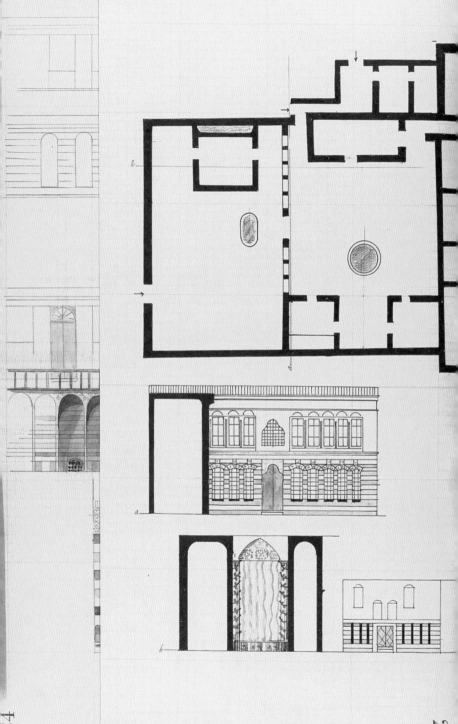

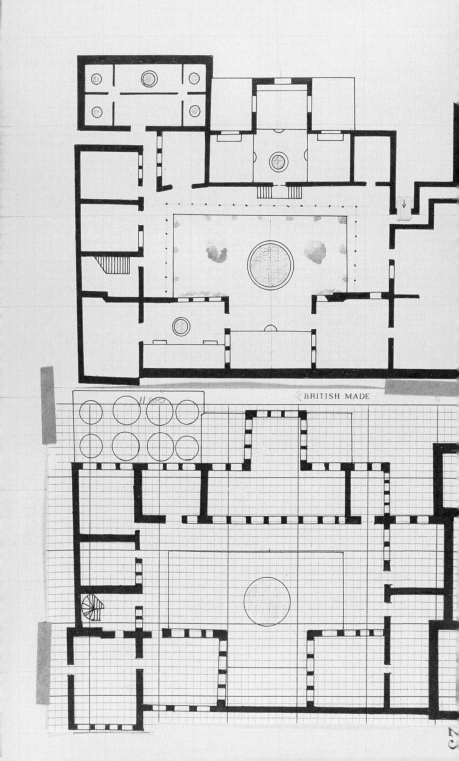

BRITISH MADE

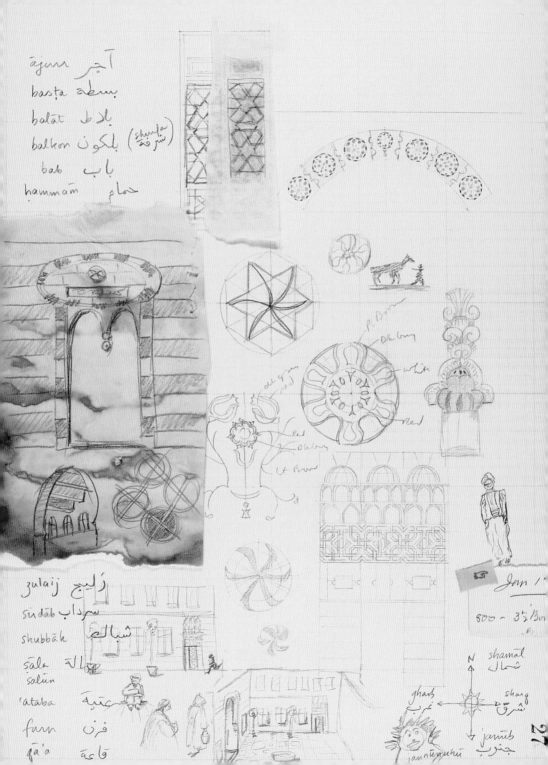

ājurr آجرّ
basṭa بسطة
balāt بلاط
balkon بلكون (sherfa شرفة)
bab باب
ḥammām حمّام

PL Brown
Dk brown
white
Red

red grn
red

red
Dk brown
Lt Brown

zulaij زليج
sirdāb سرداب
shubbāk شبّاك
ṣala صالة
salūn
'ataba عتبة
furn فرن
qā'a قاعة

Jan 1'

800 - 3½ Bo

shamal شمال
N
gharb غرب
sharq شرق
janūb جنوب
janūmuhu

27

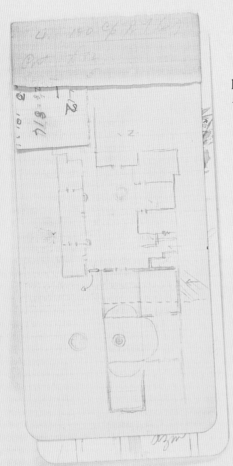

I kept on producing more fanciful sketches of houses, continuing to add details, as though I was seeing more over time. I came to realize that all along I had been endeavoring—with my sketches—to re-create the old Bait Katib from what I'd read on the walls.

When I began adding color to my work, I knew I was out of control. My palate is ordinarily limited to grays, ochers, and olives of the sort found in nature. These daubs were splattered with brilliant carmine, orange, green, blue, purple. I told myself that this bounty of form and color meant I was finally reaping the results of my studies.

Sometimes when Bait Katib seemed to spread beyond its walls, in fact, that is, not just on paper, I'd go up onto the roof to see if it was growing. Of course it wasn't, but while up there, I'd watch the comings and goings along the strip of land I'd bought adjacent to the western side. Broader than most lanes around here, it had become a public passageway, awaiting my plans to develop it. Early one evening I noticed some children playing house, the way children do, with make-believe tables and chairs. Their reenactments were elaborate, almost convincing me they were in a real salon, not one constructed out of their fantasy world. One dipped water out of an imaginary fountain; another, as the light failed, lit imaginary candles. I ran off for my notebook and returned as fast as I could. I sketched out where they had placed divans, doors, steps. When darkness fell, they pantomimed putting away dishes into nonexistent cupboards, quenching nonexistent lamps, then left, shutting a nonexistent door.

Plafond

autre?

101

marbre
terracotta

qu'a?

5m 5m 5m 5m 5m

Sinaia Bakei

I compared my hasty sketch to a drawing I had done some-time previously, one of those that had materialized from out of nowhere. It looked as though the children were playing in my illusion.

With a tape measure, chalk, the sketchbook, and a kerosene lantern, I went into the passageway. There I marked in distances and positions of features, as I had envisioned them in my own plan to see if my arrangement corresponded with the children's. It was an odd job to do in the dim, flickering light, and I was nervous lest anyone catch me at it. Surprisingly, I was left alone.

The next evening I was back on the roof, waiting for the children to return. They didn't come back that evening, nor the next. In the meantime, I anticipated needing to rechalk the lines rubbed out by the footsteps of passersby. However, except for the odd lost tourist, not a soul walked down that lane. It had been a busy shortcut, so I asked Ahmed to find out why it was being avoided.

Had I just dropped from the sky? he asked. Hadn't I heard? Not being part of the neighborhood rumor mill, unless he or Najwa chose to let me in on the gossip, of course I hadn't heard anything. He explained that an *'ifrit* had been seen—in the red-hot flames of a sorcerer's lantern—dancing and drawing magic symbols on the walls and in the air. All I had to do was go out there myself and look at the signs emblazoned all over. If I wasn't too afraid, he added.

How could I admit that this *'ifrit*, this devil, was myself? I dismissed the story with a laugh, but Ahmed was convinced. So, when I suggested—a rather cruel joke, perhaps—that it was time to incorporate the lane into the house, he nearly fainted.

I'd been worried that the children were scared off, too, but they returned a week later and resumed their play, as though the markings were more in accordance with their dreamworld than with any demon. Alas, a shopkeeper ran down the alley, gesturing wildly and pointing to the marks. The children scattered and never came back. I finally, absolutely, gave up on the idea of expanding the house.

But I haven't given up trying to determine why the west wall bothers me so. From the passageway, I regularly inspect its blank outer façade, looking for a single window, door, crack. Nothing punctures its featureless surface. From the ground up to the sky, it hides its secrets from me. These secrets have something to do with the windows looking in on my courtyard; their incompleteness haunts me.

How can I get behind the wall? How can I force it to let me in? Blind eyes always staring, refusing to reveal what they know, giving nothing away.

DAWN

JULIAN LET GO OF HIS PEN. "Blind eyes," he muttered. His head drooped to one side, his eyes closed, and his breathing became deep and heavy. He was picturing the room that he'd drawn out in such detail. It was calm in there, save for the clear, strong sound of the timeless call to prayer. How did he get into that room? He concentrated on retracing his steps back out into a tranquil courtyard and over to a painted door. This must have been the way in. His heart skipped a beat as he saw himself pushing against the door and feeling it give way then, as he stepped over the threshold and into a free fall of voices and music, urging him, pushing him toward more doors, all of which were slamming shut as he plunged past. Slamming shut, but not before revealing fleeting glimpses of a woman dressed in black, burning her as afterimages onto his retinas. He'd once told himself that he had been searching for Asilah in all the wrong places; was this, at last, the right place? All of a sudden his head jerked back, snapping him awake. "The door!" he exclaimed. He jumped up and sped across the courtyard over to the west wall.

The door was steadfast, impervious to his shoulder. He fetched a pick and a crowbar and was poised to attack it, when he changed his mind and dashed over to one of the false windows. Shielding his eyes against the glare of the rising sun, he peered through the casements, then ran his fingers over the glass and pulled at the handle. The knob came off in his hands, but the window didn't budge, for if the nails driven through the wood hadn't been enough to hold it shut, then the many layers of paint sufficed. He ran the blade of his knife between the sashes, then tried unsuccessfully to pry the window open.

Finally, he smashed the glass and reached through. His arm disappeared into an abyss, where there should have been brick.

He stood stock-still, stared at the window, then pulled at shards, madly breaking those that stuck fast. The rotting wooden lathes separating the small panes disintegrated at his touch. His hands bled, torn by the glass and his unheeding attack on it. When he'd cleared away a large opening, he pulled himself up and dove through.

Asilah

DAWN

AFRAID THAT SHE'D FRIGHTEN HIM TO DEATH or afraid that he'd turn on her, it made no difference. Fear—pure and simple—stopped Asilah from tearing Julian away from his frenzied demolition of the window. She covered her ears against his howl of pain when he smashed his hand through the glass and stared in horror as his fist collided with the wall. She gasped when he threw himself at the window, as though the brick behind it was but air.

He fell back and lay on the courtyard floor, groaning. When, after she rushed to him and helped him over to the divan, he put his hand on her arm to steady himself, she was baffled that he responded to her touch yet still did not acknowledge her.

She dampened her handkerchief in the fountain, wiped his face and hands, then rinsed out the cloth and laid it on his forehead. Knowing it was a feeble gesture but unsure what else to do, she made coffee for when he came to, placing the pot and a cup on the table beside him. He settled into steady breathing, while she paced back and forth in front of the broken window, eyeing it with each pass.

If Julian had no idea that something was hidden behind the wall, why on earth had he tried to break through it? Furthermore, how could he be the key to entering the palace, when he couldn't get into it by himself? She paused and reached through the window to touch the wall on the other side. It gave way at the light pressure of her fingers, transformed into a heavy curtain. She pushed the cloth aside and peered in to the beautiful *qa'a*. So, he had found another way in, after all.

Perhaps his notebook would reveal what he'd been thinking beforehand. She turned away from the window, glanced at the recumbent figure on the divan, then went to the study and to his notebook, now almost three-quarters full.

Because pages that had been turned before they had dried were stuck together, it was with difficulty that she found the beginning of the entry for May 27th, but when she did, the first word that caught her eye was "panic." She knew what the word meant, but it didn't make sense given the context. The dictionary didn't help either. The important thing was that it had affected his money, though she hadn't noticed any difference in the way he lived. The reference disturbed her; perhaps he couldn't afford to challenge Rafiq's claim. She opened the cupboard, shoved aside the paper encumbering its shelves, and removed a board from the back wall, uncovering a niche in which sat a small chamois bag. From it she poured a handful of gold coins onto the desk. She spread them out and counted them, stacked them neatly, then toppled them over. They were all that remained of the money her father had left her. She remembered putting them into her pocket the night she tried to leave Bait Katib, twenty years before. How long could she have lived on what they would have bought? Six months, perhaps? "They've been no use hidden away," she sighed, then pushed them aside.

In her impatience to read, she tore first one fused page, then another. Not until the very end, where he'd written about watching over the passageway and of his chalking in of the details from his sketches, did she understand his reason for smashing the window. Everything had directed him to that wall: her father's descriptions, the children's make-believe play, the trench, the locked door, she herself.

She turned the book over, found her place, and began writing, heedless of the diminishing number of pages.

وعندما يكون غائبا اقوم في بعض
الاحيان بتلوين التفاصيل - نقطة ذهبية
هنا، او لولون تركوازي هناك. والنتيجة
ساحرة بالفعل، ولا اعتقد انه يلاحظ
تلاعبي.

ويرتبط نمو المنزل ورسومه ارتباطها
متينا مع تفسيره لمز ايا الجدران. وكلما
قرأ ونقل من كلمات ابي، كلما اصبح
مسموح لي ان استكشف وبالتالي
تزداد رسوماته. ومن المحزن ان دراسته
الجدران قد وصلت الى نهايتها،
ولم يبقى، الا الجزء الذي يفتقد الى
المعاني. وليس لدي اي علم كيف
يمكن لي ان انهي هذا الامر، حيث
يجب عليه ايضا ان يتوقف، لكن
سيكون هذا امرا سهلا حيث انه ابتدأ
يرتب ذكرا في هذه المذكرات.

 ازرق
 فاروز
 خضرة
 احمر

Julian and the palace

That Julian is closely tied to the expansion of my house—as if his presence alone is responsible for its existence—is now undeniable. Each time he follows me into it, no matter how unaware of his surroundings he seems, the house grows, or what was already there becomes more lavish.

How do I know he can't see the place? Of course, I don't know for sure, but he never shows surprise or stops to inspect or touch anything, not to mention that he never notices me. But he confuses me, all the same, because every time he returns to Bait Katib he draws out what I have shown him. The most marvelous sketches flow from his pencil, often with details that I've missed. I swing between certainty of his awareness and certainty of his ignorance.

To see my incredible rooms pictured so makes them real, an assurance that I crave, as I still have difficulty believing in them myself. And I take such pleasure in watching him draw, whispering to him, "Yes, the niche looks like that," or "Unfurl the arabesque the other way." Sometimes, in his absence, I color in the details; a touch of gilt here, a dab of turquoise there. The results are admirable, and I don't think he notices my interference.

Both the expansion of the house and his drawings are closely tied with his translation of the wall. The more that he reads and transcribes of my father's words, the more I am allowed to discover and the more he draws. Sadly, the translation has come to an end. Only the blank patch remains. I'm at as much of a loss of how to finish this as he must be, though it will be easier now that he's organizing his years here in this journal.

جوليان والقصر

وليسى هنالك بين شك ان وجود جوليان اصبح مرتبطاً قوياً مع مجريات اتساع منزلي، كلما لون وجوده اصبح السبب في وجود هذا المنزل. وكلما يتبعني، وبالرغم من عدم ادراكه المحيط الذي يقع حواليه، يستمر المنزل في الاتساع، والاشياء التي كانت موجودة، تصبح اكثر ترفخامة وجمالا.

وكيف اعرف انه لايرى المكان؟ بالطبع اني غير متأكدة من ذلك، لكنه لايبدو عليه ابداً الشعور بالمفاجأة، ولايقف ليلمس ويتحسس الاشياء، وبالتأكيد انه لايراني. النه مع ذلك يحيرني، حيث انه كلما يعود الى "بيت كاتب"، يرسم ما يبقى. ان رسوم قلمه جميلة جداً، رسوم بالبيئة بالتفاصيل التي فاتت واتقلب بين تخيلي انه يعلم بوجودي جهله لذلك الوجود.

... ما أرى ان مجراتي الخيالية ترسم على الورق، اصبحت اقرب من بحقيقة وجودها، واتطلع الى ان تكون هذه

ومن دواعي سروري العظيمة هو مراقبتي اياه وهويرسم في اذنه شكلها كذا" نعم هذه النقوش... او "ارم الزاوية الترفخامة باتجاه اخر."

MORNING

ASILAH CHECKED ON JULIAN, who was now sleeping soundly, sprawled on his back. She stood by him quietly, willing him to wake up and see her. Instead, he rolled over on his side, his back to her, and sighed deeply.

There was nothing more she could do here; it was time to return to her own house. She heaved herself up and over the sill of the broken window, dropped down into the *qa'a*, and instinctively walked up the steps leading up to one of the platforms. When she pulled back a cushion, she could see chalk marks on the wall. Was she living in Julian's illusion or was he living in hers?

Julian

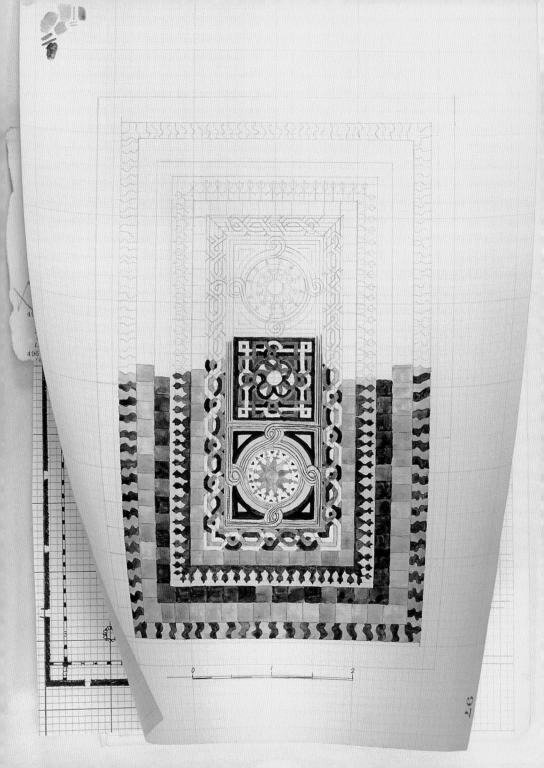

Afternoon

His head and hands wrapped in gauze—the work of the infirmary—Julian grasped his pen and made a few tentative strokes. "Not too bad," he said, wincing at the pain the effort caused. He set the pen down and brushed his bandaged hand against the pile of coins he only just noticed. With difficulty, he picked up one between his thumb and forefinger and examined it closely. It seemed to be of gold.

Its surfaces were worn almost smooth—presumably from much handling—but he could make out a sultan's *tughra*, or signature, on one side, and a date—A.H. 1255—on the other.

He got up and studied the spines of the books on the shelves opposite. Finding the one he was looking for, he took it down and went back to his desk. In a few minutes he had identified the coins as Ottoman medjidies, dating from the first year of the reign of Abdul Aziz in 1861.

He lined up the coins across the top of the desk, counted forty-seven of them, their denominations ranging from 100 to 500 piastres. Their monetary value was immaterial. That they were sitting on his desk when he was all alone in the house was enough to convince him that he was precariously positioned on the brink of dementia. "There is no one else here." His words, spoken out loud, emphasized his solitude. He sat immobile, staring, then picked up a pencil and traced out the design, first of one side, then of the other as though, by drawing, he would justify their existence. He finally swept up the coins and put them in his trouser pocket, where their bulk sat comfortably heavy.

May 28th, 1945

I am now in possession of a small fortune in antique coins; how, I don't know, unless it's my house spirit taking care of me, worried that I don't have the means to pay for my appeal. I did ask her for help. This shows she's been listening.

I must break my account to mention my experience of last night or, rather, this morning. Some delusion drove me to smash a courtyard window. In the process, I cut up my hands rather badly and reopened the wound on the back of my head. I can't say what made me do it——. No, I know perfectly well what made me do it; the blind windows and the door goaded me. I've been so obstinately and irrationally focused on that wall, that I imagine it has the answers to all my foolish questions. It's only two feet thick; there is nothing but a passageway behind it. It hides nothing, no secret rooms, no Asilah. I tell myself this again and again, yet I feel life pulsating within it, pulling me in, as though I have something to do with that life, that I'm a part of it. But I'm ashamed of my behavior. Attacking an inanimate building is sheer bloody-mindedness. It's resulted in nothing but damage, which I'll have to fix, and a dream: a dream of the fabulous house I've been so obsessed with over the years.

In my dream, I crawled into the house through the window, crossed a room shimmering with thousands of tiny mirrors, and walked out into the courtyard. Everything was so familiar, each feature where I envisioned it. I was drawn to ascend a set of stairs that led to another room. The room was extraordinary; it was the room I had imagined and sketched. The panels were painted the same colors, the ceiling was as intricate, even the play of light was the same. I circled round the *'ataba*, studying the three platforms. From the pattern of the brocade to the position of the cushions and the overlap of the carpets, they matched the palace perfectly. In my mind, I checked off the contents of the closed cupboards, then went and opened each of them. Nothing was out of place.

On one of the platforms was a small inlaid table, upon which had been set a coffeepot and a cup. The coffee was hot. I sat down on the divan and took a sip, savoring the bitterness of the cardamom and feeling every bit like that girl, Alice, in the children's story. Nothing happened. Why would it? I'd already fallen into my wonderland. Then I must have dozed off. I mean, I was already asleep, but in my dream, I must have dozed off. When I woke up, I was lying on the divan in my own *liwan*, a damp and bloody cloth on the pillow, and a coffeepot and a cup on the table next to me. Except for the sludge of grounds, both pot and cup were empty.

My head hurt like hell; the walls spun round as I stood up. Scratches and cuts scored my hands, glass was strewn across the courtyard floor. The wall behind the window was solid brick. It's easy to see that I never went into that room, but I certainly destroyed the window. And where did the coffee come from?

Where's Halabi? I'd have gone to his office myself, if I hadn't needed to get patched up. Tomorrow is Tuesday, the 29th of May. Just two days to go. I'm so tired. I might as well continue on with my history, but after I've had some sleep.

العشاء

EVENING

1936 until present

1936 stands out, if only because of the general strike. From the 20th of January until the end of February, in the midst of frigid temperatures and brutal winds that froze me to the very core of my being, the bazaars were shut down. Given that I spent those days huddled in front of the cold, unlit oven, wrapped in a quilt, daydreaming of a crackling hot fire, I was amazed that anyone could function, not to mention organize a strike. It was an astonishing reaction to the forced closure of the National Bloc's offices and the arrest of Barudi, followed by the killing of four protestors by French troops near the Umayyad Mosque. In retaliation—and from the warmth of his centrally heated office, no doubt—the PM announced that the strike would last until the constitution was restored. This was all very well as far as principles go, if it weren't for the unbearable suffering of the merchants and us customers who couldn't buy necessities like fuel.

It was a confusing time and well worth ignoring if you ask me, though it wasn't as bad as the reports we hear about Europe's war with Hitler. We'd been left alone until 1940 when the pro-Vichy General Dentz was appointed High Commissioner. All of a sudden, Germans were allowed to land their aircraft in Syria, which, naturally, pleased neither the British nor the Free French. They joined forces and successfully invaded during the summer of 1941, confronting the Vichy to the west of the city. The Allies bravely shielded themselves with Australian and British Indian troops, while the Vichy hid behind North Africans. The not-so-distant bombs awoke bad memories for a lot of us, but the action was mercifully short-lived.

Of course, the Allies never trusted each other, nor should they have. The Brits were aiming to increase their influence in Syria, and the French were conspiring to stay put. It looks like France will clear off any day, though no one knows how the transfer of power will play out. There've been anti-French demonstrations here this past week.

I suppose I can't avoid writing about my own state of affairs. For me, personally, this period was one of death. It was to be expected; I had surrounded myself with old folk. The first to go was Burhan Efendi. He'd been coming over every Tuesday, but the better my Arabic got, the shorter the time he would stay, till one day he didn't show up. I asked around and was told that he'd had a mild stroke, so I went over to his house where I found him sitting up in bed, wearing a pair of flannel pajamas printed with large damask roses. He fumbled for something to throw over the ridiculous garment, grabbing his wife's bed shawl, a lacy, indeed racy, little item. I stood looking at him as he scowled and harumphed, then was struck by the goddamnedest thing; the stroke had evened out his features. I had to laugh at his pajamas, his newly symmetrical face, the silly shawl, but mostly I laughed in relief that he was well enough to be embarrassed.

Unfortunately, he wasn't able to resume the lessons so, till his death five years ago, I stopped by to see him every Tuesday. He was in his seventies, though his long white beard and his forehead crisscrossed with countless wrinkles made him look older.

It was Ahmed's death in 1942 that hit the hardest, yet he was the oldest, at least eighty-two, probably older. In truth, he looked eighty when we first met at Beramke station twenty years ago.

How can I write about Ahmed's death? Yet he died so easily, slipping away like a silent puff of smoke. On the morning of August the 10th, a Monday—generally considered a day of good luck—he stayed in his room. This was so out of character that I went to his door and called him. When there was no

Ahmad 1928
Bait Hatch

answer, I looked in and saw him lying on his back, his kif pipe on his chest. I assumed he was still asleep. He'd been fine, no creakier than usual, and eating well. I decided to let him be. Until ten, that is. This was scandalously late; he'd never slept more than two hours past the dawn call to prayer. I went over to his bed and looked at him more closely. There was no mistaking the pallor, the immobility. I put my hand on his forehead, more for the last chance to touch him than to confirm what I already knew. By sunset he was buried, wearing his clean Friday turban.

I fought with myself about whether or not to let him take his pipe, but he had nothing else to leave me, so I kept it. Najwa and I were the only mourners. He'd outlasted everyone else.

Najwa died last year—of a tumor that apparently had been slowly eating away at her. She was sixty-nine, respectably old for a woman who had borne five children and whose life was marked by sacrifice. And the only photograph that I'd ever found of Asilah was buried with her before I had a chance to get it back.

I sat with her invalid husband every evening through the period of mourning, insensibly grieving the loss of the photograph. Her son, Shukri, the one who had been involved in the revolt and was now a big wheel in the cement business, would stay for a little while. He couldn't understand why I was there, and it was beyond me to explain.

It wasn't until I had no more dour evenings ahead of me that it hit me how great the loss of Najwa really was. Not only was she my sole link to Asilah, but I had come to love her deeply. By way of a joke I called her *Oum Baiti*, or "mother of my house," and she'd whack me with her broom, or mop, or whatever she had in her hand. But she was pleased, I know now. She told all of her friends; when they greeted me, it was by *Ibn Oum al-Bait*, "son of the mother of the house." In spite of our affection for each other, though, I don't doubt that when she died, some part of her still accused me of causing Asilah's disappearance.

NIGHT

EVER SINCE AMIN AL-RAFIQ UPSET JULIAN'S WORLD, DUST—
a plentiful commodity in Damascus—had begun accumulating,
and Julian had made only a trifling attempt to sweep away foot-
prints and leaves, not to mention the pile of broken glass from
the window. Without Najwa's ministrations, cobwebs were
already hanging from the high ceilings; mice were nesting in the
kitchen. The city was exerting its own claims upon his house,
creeping in slowly but unmistakably. An impulse to tidy up
drove him to find a mop and pail. The moon, though bright, was
insufficient to illuminate the courtyard, so he lit the lanterns.
Their gentle glow gave a festive atmosphere. He laughed with a
giddy energy, ran into his study, and put on a record by
Muhyiddin Ba'yun. To the hypnotic notes of the *tanbur*, he
dipped the pail in the fountain's basin, then realized he'd
forgotten soap. Not finding any in the storeroom or the kitchen,
he grabbed a torch and descended into the cellar.

The sound of the two-stringed lute echoed hauntingly
through the cellar, seemingly coming from all directions. He
shone the torch over the shelves laden with sun-dried tomatoes
and apricots, dried herbs, and bars of Aleppo soap. As the music
ended, a dark shadow on the wall beyond the shelving caught his
eye. Forgetting his chore, he stepped over to the spot, aimed his
light on it and patted the clay. A stain in the soil that he'd never
noticed before had tricked him into seeing an opening. The same
kind of discoloration had formed on the other three walls.
Concerned that dampness was leaching into the ground and
undermining the foundations, he tapped each one. The soil was
dry and hard. Reassured, he thought no more of them. Soap in
hand, he climbed back up to the courtyard.

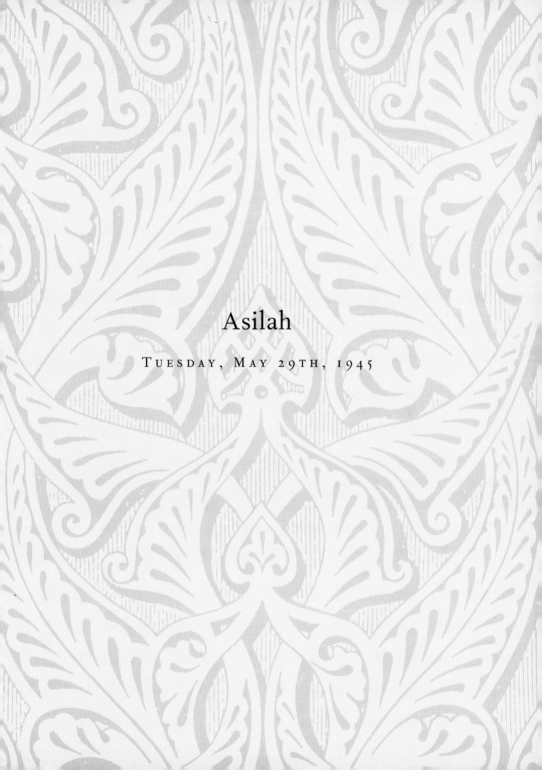

Asilah

Night

HIDDEN DEEPLY WITHIN HERSELF, Asilah followed Julian down into Bait Katib's cellar, now a huge cavern from which four vaulted tunnels radiated. Where has this come from? she asked herself, gaping at the massive space. She watched Julian pause at the shelves, then walk over to one of the openings, taking surprisingly few steps to cross what appeared to be a great distance. He shone his light upon it and passed his hand across it, but he didn't step into it. He pivoted around and did the same thing at the other three entrances. Finally, he turned away, took something off a shelf, and climbed back up the stairs to the courtyard.

When he was out of sight, she considered each of the entrances. Loud voices and laughter echoed through the first one, directly in front; music could be heard from the second, on the left; the third, behind, emitted the gurgle of trickling water; wind whistled down the fourth, on the right. She chose the one in front, whence came voices, and plunged into it, feeling her way tentatively. The earth was firm below her feet. She took a few cautious steps. Then a few more, right into a spider's web. "Puah!" she cried, as she scraped at the sticky threads with her fingernails. Something farther along scuttled away. It seemed to take hours to traverse the tunnel's length, when it couldn't have been more than a few minutes. At the far end she ascended a set of stairs and walked out into a *haramlik*, awash with the bright sunshine of midday. A current of icy air passed through her, as though she had stepped into a room that had been too long unvisited.

The voices she'd heard were those of a cluster of women, all dressed in ankle-length silk robes with intricately embroidered bodices. Around their waists were multicolored belts; from their necks hung chains of gold. They were laughing and gossiping, sitting or strolling, playing with children.

"Hello," she called out, but no one replied or even glanced in her direction. A woman ambling past brushed her arm. "Excuse me," said Asilah but got no response. She was surprised that she could walk around unheeded. Yet, there was something about them that came from so far away that she realized she wasn't in the least surprised.

Upon inspection, the courtyard looked awfully like Bait Katib's. True, the tapestries and furniture were of a different style, the flowers were not kinds she had planted, and the fruit trees were smaller, less mature, but the similarities were remarkable, nonetheless. Something was missing, though. At first she couldn't put her finger on it, then she noticed. There were no electric lights! One of the most magical moments of her childhood had been the installation of electricity. The family had invited everyone in the quarter to celebrate the occasion. But that wasn't the only thing missing. Whatever it is, she told herself, this must be another house that replicates Bait Katib almost exactly, from the painted ceiling in the *liwan* to the placement of the doors and windows. But all the same, it was too familiar. Had she stepped into Bait Katib's living past? She shivered with the idea that such a thing could be possible; yet was it so very different from rebuilding a long-gone Bait Katib, as she had done? Yes, it was, she decided. Her palace consisted of the unfamiliar; this place was like a distorted dream of her very existence.

As she walked toward the door that would lead to the next courtyard, her surroundings dimmed, becoming indistinct, like a photograph left out in the sun. Fearful that she, too, would fade, she stopped and turned around.

She noticed a narrow, shallow canal running through the middle of the courtyard. Like the canal described in the chronicle on the wall, this canal erupted from a hole in one wall and disappeared down a drain in the floor on the opposite side. One of the women cried out gleefully as a tray filled with sweetmeats came floating along the stream. Another woman, who had the appearance of a maid, knelt down and grabbed the tray. Asilah had never seen this means of serving cloistered women. Barely able to make out any more details through the fog of time that had settled on the place, she left them picking at the tidbits, still unsure of what she had just witnessed.

Back in the cellar, she chose the tunnel from which music could be heard playing. This one took her a shorter time to traverse and gave way to the same courtyard, or almost the same. Now a solitary young woman sat in the *liwan*, picking out notes on an oud. Ignoring the woman as she herself was ignored, she noted that subtle changes had been made from the previous courtyard, the whitewash was a different shade, but there was something else——. A ladder leaned against one of the walls; tools and a bucket of plaster sat on the floor. Above the ladder was a patch of relief work, Arabic script impressed into gesso-duro. Were these her fathers words? From when he first began his history? Oh, what a fabulous dream this is! she thought.

She clapped her hands in delight, then looked closely at the woman. Mother? she whispered. The woman did not acknowledge her and kept on playing. Asilah tiptoed across the courtyard and stood close. Mother? she spoke louder this time, but still the woman did not respond. Asilah sat down; the body that she put her arm around was there, and it wasn't—as was, and wasn't, the shoulder she rested her head upon. The music came from far away. If only I didn't have to go, she thought, if only I could stay here forever, I'd be able to start all over again, without the revolt, without the deaths. She looked at the woman sitting by her side. You are my mother, aren't you? Her words had no sound but echoed strongly in her head. But so young, before you became a mother. Perhaps that's why you don't see me. I don't exist. Yet. She kissed the woman's cheeks and forehead, and as she did so the fingers picking the oud's strings faltered ever so slightly.

Before Asilah returned to the tunnel, she looked up at the deep blue sky. The sun was low.

The third tunnel, from which she heard the trickling water, took hardly any time to walk through and led to the courtyard of present-day Bait Katib. Julian had rolled up the legs of his trousers and was sitting on the rim of the basin, dangling his feet in the water. He was holding the key to the old, large door and was humming to himself. The wall was now entirely finished, even the part that she knew was still not complete. She skirted the fountain, squinting as she walked toward the wall, trying to read the final words that Julian must have just written. They kept going out of focus as though the plaster had been written over several times before it had dried. The shapes were right but she couldn't concentrate on them, even when she knelt down and examined them closely. She looked up and blinked hard. Swallows were zigzagging across the darkening sky, which was edged with the brilliant pinks and purples of the setting sun. What did the wall say? Would she ever find out?

She was reluctant to go along the fourth and final tunnel, from which came nothing but the sound of wind. Finally, she dashed up it so quickly she couldn't remember doing so. She came out into an expanse of weeds and convulsed marble slabs surrounded by mounds of crumbled bricks. Harsh moonlight cast long shadows. Nothing stirred. Of all the courtyards this was the least like Bait Katib's yet felt the most inevitable.

Julian

Tuesday, May 29th, 1945

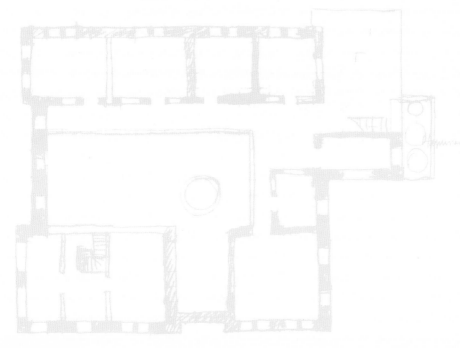

Late Morning

The knocking was brisk and businesslike. Julian ran down the stairs and over to the door, where he was handed an envelope and a long-stemmed rose by a porter so elegant in dress and so dignified in manner that Julian, fingering the coins in his pocket, forgetting they were gold, hesitated to offer him a tip. When at last he held out one, the porter politely refused it.

Before stepping back into the house, Julian studied the porter, who was now walking down the street. Dressed in voluminous Turkish trousers, an embroidered vest, and *babouche*, or slippers, with toes curled like Aladdin's lamps, he could have easily been part of a sultan's entourage. The medjidie coin wouldn't have been at all out of place. When the man reached the end of the street, he glanced back and smiled, then vanished round the corner.

Julian walked to the *liwan*, absently tearing open the envelope. He flopped down on the divan to read the letter. It was from Halabi. The lawyer wrote that the strike had prevented him from making any headway with the appeal, but he had assurances from a prosecutor acquaintance that, under the circumstances, no eviction could take place on May 30th, though he certainly couldn't guarantee that an effort wouldn't be made.

In the meantime, he added, if you care to look at the enclosure, you will see details of Asilah Katib's death. Julian's heart stopped, then began pounding wildly. He read on. Not official, of course, the lawyer underlined, but the best that can be reconstructed from the records of the time. A surge of heat ricocheted through the veins of Julian's neck and raced along his ears and across his cheeks. Tears flooded his eyes; he let them spill.

After twenty years of searching for this very proof, of denying this possibility, Halabi had cleared it up in a mere four days. The details were sparse. Asilah's body had been taken to the Nur ad-Din hospital on the morning of October 19th, 1925. Her address was marked unknown, though it was noted that she was retrieved from nearby. She was identified as being "about twenty." Julian mentally corrected that detail; she had been twenty-nine. She had been shot. The surgeon had counted eighteen bullet wounds. It was claimed that an effort had been made to contact her family but, in the confusion of those days, the attempt was doubtless cursory, probably limited to posting a notice—among hundreds of others—at the hospital's entrance. Her possessions were itemized: articles of clothing, a fragment of a poem signed by Nasim Katib, and forty-seven gold coins. Julian picked up the rose, which he'd placed on the divan, and inhaled deeply. This one had no fragrance whatsoever.

He counted the coins again—forty-seven—then tossed one of them into the air. "Heads," he called out. He caught it and held it in his closed fist. When he opened the hand, still smarting from the cuts, he had no idea which side was which. "I win," he said and got up from the divan.

"I win," he repeated, as he walked out from the shade to the edge of the fountain. "I win what?" He flipped the coin into the water—it barely created a ripple—then stretched out over the basin and stared intently at his reflection. "This is the part in the fairy tale where the maiden peers over my shoulder," he laughed, but stopped suddenly, disturbed by the strident peal of hysteria underlying his laughter. He dipped his head into the coolness, stood up, and shook himself like a wet dog.

"Don't be an ass," he scolded himself. "You know she's dead. Prove to yourself that you know it." He marched up the stairs and toward the room in which she had once slept. The door was slightly ajar. "Damn it, I told you to keep it closed!" he shouted, grabbing the knob and wrenching it shut. The bang startled and shamed him. He reopened it quietly, leaving it as he had found it. And continued to walk, a determined yet restless walk with no apparent purpose, no possible destination.

He'd spent so many years wavering between certainty of her death and belief in her survival. At what point had he lost his conviction that she was dead? Out of what delusion came the impressions of her existence? Whispers, perfume, melodies? The stuff of fantasy. Or was it because of his faith in Najwa's belief? Right up to the day she passed away, Najwa had watched the door, expecting Asilah to walk through it.

Julian studied the death certificate again. Eighteen bullet holes, the doctor had counted. Why is this so tragic to me? he asked himself. I lived through three years of this and worse. But he knew it was pointless to compare tragedies; it was all an insane waste.

His world had become so muddled, out of step. He'd just spent the better part of two decades looking for a stranger who, in the course of time, had become the most important person in his life. To discover that he would never meet her again, after devoting so much to her, was crushing beyond belief. He thought back over the years. What else had he done? He had tried to substitute another life, another history, for his own, and failed. He'd learned to think in a language that defied straight lines and logic. And he'd sacrificed reams of paper in the pointless execution of plans and sketches of a nonexistent house.

What could explain those sketches of the fabulous rooms? Catching himself rubbing the back of his head, he shuddered to a stop. It was his shrapnel-riddled brain; it must be. Nothing had been right since the injury. He'd been creating these illusions all by himself, abetted by the magical sights and sounds of Damascus and by the layered history of the house in which he lived.

He breathed deeply with the relief of having found a rational explanation, ruefully touching the scar tissue once again. "There," he said, "no need to get fussed." He returned to his study, determined to add Halabi's information to his notebook, and turned to a new page, pen poised. He froze. The page was already filled—as was the one facing it—with writing in Arabic. He flipped rapidly through to the end. It was all crammed full. Some flower petals fell out onto his lap, others had gummed the pages together. Before carefully turning the book over, he raised it and breathed in the pages, the perfume of the flowers mixing with the reassuring stink of glue and paint. Then he read the first line, "The day Julian arrived," and snapped the book shut, his clumsy fingers unable to close the cover fast enough. He couldn't breathe. He spun around and threw the shutters open. The air outside was leaden and hot.

He got up. It was easier to leave than to confront the writing. But he sank back down and opened the book again. A few more lines convinced him that he was reading Asilah's words. By the end of the page, he was barely able to remain seated. He had begun nervously folding and unfolding the pages; he again rubbed the scar on the back of his head, but this time his fingernails gouged the skin. The realness of the pain brought him a measure of calm, allowing him to concentrate on Asilah. She wasn't dead after all. But then, where did Halabi's information come from? He could resist the notebook no longer; he read it to the end, then closed it.

He walked out into the courtyard and studied the blank space on the wall. Now I know what to write, he whispered. When the air is cooler. When I can think straight. From his position in the

عليها للنثر و بدى لي انها اجمل قاعة رأيتها
~~الى الجو والذي سوخيلوس طلو~~ في حياتي.
و غطست قد مي في السجادة الحريرية
~~طر~~ التي انعكست نقو شها على طلاء
الجدر ان . وتحسست يدي ظفيرة
من الذهب. وقادني بعض الضؤ الذي
انعكس من الظفيرة الى شبابيك خلف
كل منضة، وكل منها عاطية بزخرفة ولها
مشربية عريضة تتسع الجلوس عليها.
وانتقل نظري من الشبابيك الى السقف
الذي امتلئ بالنقوش المرسومة عليه .
ولم تكن الا لواح والعوارض الخشبية
تعكس رسومات السجاد او تضم رسوم
لحقول الزهور، الن كل واحد منها كان
منقوشا برسوم بيوت ومعابد. ومناظر
طبيعية وجنائن، والازض والسماء.
وتحول خيالي الى حاكي القصص
الذي يتنقل بين مدن سرية.
وعند الخط الذي يربط بين السقف
والجدران كانت هناك نقوش تشابه
خلايا النحل بينها الواح كتب عليها
بيوت من الشعر بأيدي خطاط توازي

ولم يبد وان هناك مخرج اخر، ولو دخل
الى لجرة الرآني. وخياري الوحيد هو ان
اختبأ، لكن اين؟ وكان في لجرة ثلاث
منصات، كل واحدة منها بارتفاع درجة
عن العتبة. وقفزت الى المنصة التي على
يساري واسرعت الى خزانة بنيت في
الحائط وفي نيتي ان ازحف اليها الآن
جوليان دخل لجرة قبل ان اصل اليها
والقى نظرة سريعة حول الجرة متجاهلا
اياي وكذلك محيطه، وخرج لتوه.
وتداعيت بسجدي على الديوان وهززت
رأسي مستغربتا. هل الجنية؟ وقرصت
رسغي الى ان اوجعني كلا. ان الارواح
لاتشعر بالالم، وليست الأرواح بحاجة
لان تفتح ابوان او الدخول من خلالها، -
ووقفت متطلعة الى اثر البقعة التي
تركتها على الديوان - لاتترك الارواح
اثارا على الافرشة. فأمن المكن اني في عالم
اخر؟ انه عالم جميل ان كنت في الحقيقة
في عالم اخر.
ونظرت مرة اخرى الى داخل لجرة لاتعرف

لماذا ارهاني؟

center of the courtyard, he slowly revolved, studying some distant point in front of him as he turned. Where are you? he asked, in the same low whisper. He recommenced walking.

It was so stifling. Only the roof offered even a slight breeze. He leaned over the western edge and tried to visualize where he had drawn the chalk marks long since effaced by rain and snow. A distant drone of airplanes caught his attention. He looked up but could see nothing. Moving back from the edge, fearing for his balance, he scoured the sky. The sun burned into him, and he became aware of a growing discomfort behind his left ear. The reopened wound was throbbing as if the shrapnel in his skull was a conductor for the heat and the noise. A sudden stabbing pain sent him lurching across the roof. Power drained out of his legs. Barely upright, he skidded down the stairs and into the courtyard.

The house caved in toward him. It straightened up when he shook his head, an illusion brought on by the pain. The hum of the airplanes was now a distinct whine. Wherever they were, they were flying low and getting closer.

Suddenly, he had the appalling sensation that he was the only person left in Damascus. Claustrophobic and frightened, he saw no alternative but to flee, but in his panic, he ran to the wrong door and pushed it open. That it gave way startled him only when he emerged into the courtyard Asilah had first lured him into so many years before.

But this time, he could see it. He stopped dead in his tracks and stared at the unfamiliar familiar place. He could no longer hear the airplanes, his headache had vanished, his legs had regained their strength, the air was soft and cool. Leaning against the rim of the fountain was a young woman with thick, straight brown hair and black eyes. She smiled at him, but when he walked toward her with a quizzical look in his face, her smile faded, replaced with a questioning frown.

He stopped and cautiously held his hand out to her, clearly not believing what he was seeing. His fingers, lightly, tentatively, grazed her face, but instead of the firmness it promised, its skin was as fragile and ephemeral as a dragonfly's wing. Looking at her more closely, he saw scars cutting across her cheek and forehead. Underlying her healthy glow was the disturbing sallowness of illness or neglect.

"You can see me?" Her voice seemed to come from far away. She rested her own hand on his, as though she, too, couldn't believe he was real. Her fingers that were full and shapely, felt unexpectedly lean. Still clasping his hand, she stood up. "Why?" she asked. "Why now?" From her came the rustle of parchment. Her amber scent could not mask the bite of ancient dust.

Julian looked uneasily around the courtyard, taking in all of the details. "I've seen this place before, somewhere—. I know. My drawings. I drew this out."

"You've been here before," she assured him, softly. "You just couldn't see it then. But why now?" she repeated, shaking her head. A shiver ripped through her. Louder, she said, "But, what am I thinking of, I must show you what you've helped me build." Her voice strengthened, as though she was accustoming herself to speaking out loud, or her voice was finding the body it belonged to. She led him into the *qa'a*. They stood in silence, staring at the gorgeous room.

"I helped you build this? What do you mean?" he finally asked.

"I was hoping you could tell me." She pulled him over to the window. "What do you make of this?" They looked out over a lively Damascus street from the distant past.

He had dreamed of finding Asilah and of discovering the source of his inspiration for the drawings. And now he had found both, but never had he imagined that by doing so he would be stepping outside his place, his time. It was too much to take in.

He closed his eyes hard. If I keep them like this for long enough, he told himself, everything will be normal again. He opened them to the same scene. "Where exactly are we?" he asked.

"Where do you think?" she responded.

"Bait Katib?"

She nodded, then said, "But a Bait Katib of another age." She led him through the other rooms. He recognized every one of them but lost himself all the same in rediscovering them: the scriptorium and library, the *hammam*, the salons. In his wonder at the marvelous palace and his joy at being with Asilah, he understood that it didn't matter if time wasn't as it seemed. He had what he wanted.

As they returned along an arcaded corridor he was startled to find candles now lit. He looked at her questioningly. She shrugged; who lit them was a mystery she had never solved.

"Come back with me, help me finish the wall." He gestured toward the door.

"No," she pulled away. "Not yet." She did not add that she would never go back there.

"But you have to read what I've written; I'm almost finished."

She shook her head. "I've read it. Now that we're both here, we must stay." She sat down on the rim of the fountain.

Julian sat next to her. "Why didn't you ever tell me you were here?"

"I couldn't. I thought you would make me leave. I had nowhere else to go."

"You must have known that I would never have turned you away. Not for anything in the world. Didn't you see how I kept your home for you? And now, do you realize we're about to lose it?"

She looked at him and said, "I don't think anyone will take Bait Katib away from us. No one will get it."

The sensation that he wouldn't be leaving after all washed over Julian. It was all taken care of, it was her house, it could belong to no one else. A heavy weight lifted from his shoulders, a weight that he hadn't even recognized was there. But the one thing left to do had to be done before he would be completely free.

He stood up. "Help me with the wall. I promised Nasim I'd finish it, and I almost have. There's just a small spot left." He put his arm around her to lead her to the old house. For a dizzying moment, he thought he saw his hand through her body. But the moment passed, and they walked toward the door. As they neared it, she again hesitated.

"No, don't go out there. We're safer here. My father would understand."

"I must go back," he said to her. "Now that I've found you, I must. To finish the wall. Please come with me. It won't take long." His arm still around her, he stepped into Bait Katib's courtyard. But as he walked, certain that she was by his side, he realized that he'd left her behind. He turned around and saw her standing at the door, frantically beckoning him to return. The door began to swing shut, but she pushed it and struggled to hold it open. She called out to him.

"I'll be right back," he replied. "I must finish the wall," he repeated under his breath, as though to reassure himself that he was doing what had to be done.

In the short passage between the one courtyard and the other, night had fallen. The sound of airplanes again filled the air. There were two of them directly overhead. He covered his ears with his hands, the headache was back, worse than before. Where were the stars bursting from? Not stars. Flashes of man-made constellations. More airplanes flew over, then suddenly a deafening whistling rent the sky, followed by a thunderous crash.

A gush of air pulled his gaze to a gaping hole in the court-yard wall. A shell had hit the house. Flames already consuming the exposed wood and straw were spreading fast. A man was slumped on the marble tiles near the hole. Not thinking of who this stranger was or how he got there, Julian rushed over to him to drag him to safety but hesitated when he saw blood flowing from a wound on the back of the man's head. He put his hand on the man's neck but could feel no pulse. He looked at the wall; the man had been writing on it, writing on the smooth surface that Nasim had left blank. Julian quickly scanned the new text. It was a scribbled account of Asilah's last hours. Her unsuc-cessful attempt to escape the bombardment; her effort to save the boy, Selim; the hail of bullets that cut her down. Then her last memory, the hands that felt her neck, her heart, for her pulse, that pulled her off Selim's body and carried her into darkness. The words ended abruptly with the destruction of the house. The man was still grasping the thick reed pen with which he had been writing.

Julian involuntarily rubbed his own head and realized that the pain was gone, then he rolled the body over and looked himself in the face. He stood up, turned his back to the wall, and walked toward Asilah, who was still pushing against the door, pleading with him to hurry. As he reached her, the house shim-mered and burned, then disintegrated, leaving nothing but blackened, overgrown ruins.

انفجار فنبلة على حريقة

◆◆◆

دمشق : السبت في الثاني من تموز ١٩٤٥. خلال الهجوم على دمشق من قبل القوات الجوية الفرنسية في ٢٩ و ٣٠ ايار القيت عبوة ياسفة على منطقة حريقة اصابت بناية قديمة مهجورة انحصرت الخسائر على أطراف البنايات القديمة. أحد الجيران المدعو «يونس استاز» يقول فضلا للخرافات القديمة بقيت بعيدة عن الانظار. الأرض كانت قديما معروفة تحت اسم «بيت كاتب» وقد هدمت خلال حريقة سنة ١٩٢٥. خلاف عائلي قد أخر اعادة تعميره.

BOMBARDEMENT À DAMAS

Vendredi, 1er juin 1945, Damas : Dans la soirée du 29 mai, et jusqu'au midi le lendemain, les forces aériennes françaises ont bombardé Damas, dans un effort pour réprimer le sentiment anti-français. Le bâtiment visé était le Parlement, dans le quartier de Salhiyya. Un obus a été accidentellement lâché sur le quartier de Hariqa, qui avait déjà subi des dégâts importants en octobre 1925. Notre correspondant nous apprend que l'obus est tombé sur un terrain vague et qu'il n'y a pas eu de pertes en vies humaines.

(Suite page 6, col. 1)

Le quartier de Hariqa, qui a

'Alif Ba
Bomb Hits Hariqa
Saturday, June 2nd, 1945, Damascus: In the attack of Damascus by the French airforce on May 29th and 30th, a missile dropped over the Hariqa quarter in the Old City landed in a vacant lot. Damage was limited to the walls of the adjacent buildings. One of the neighbors, Yunis Ustaz, spoke of how it was lucky an old superstition kept people away from the spot.

The property was once the location of a house, known as Bait Katib, which had been destroyed during the burning of Hariqa in 1925. A family dispute had delayed rebuilding on the site.

Les Échos de Syrie
Bombs Hit Damascus
Friday, June 1st, 1945, Damascus: French forces bombarded Damascus from the evening of May 29th until noon the following day, in an effort to quell anti-French sentiment. The target was the Parliament building in the Salhiyya district. One missile was accidentally released over the Hariqa district, which had seen extensive damage in October 1925. Reports indicate that it landed in a vacant property and that no lives were lost.

ACKNOWLEDGMENTS

The author wishes to thank everyone who offered guidance, information, and inspiration: Brigid Keenan, author of *Damascus: Hidden Treasures of the Old City*, for her generosity and for opening so many Damascus doors; Fatie Darwish, for bringing Damascus's past to life; Rabie al-Darra, Hassahn Zahabi, Dr. Sultan Ali, and Hakam Dandy, for sharing their knowledge of the city and its history; Alan Sillitoe, for the much-appreciated deluge of Damascus maps; Laurent Budik, for the invaluable reference material; Todd Belcher, for the assistance with the photography; Liz Darhansoff, for her encouragement; Sarab Atassi-Khattab, Hayma Zifa, and Muhammad al-Dbiyat of the Institut Français d'Études Arabes de Damas (IFEAD), Damascus, for their time, knowledge, and enthusiasm; Les Archives du Centre d'Études de Photographes du Moyen-Orient (ACEPMO), Paris, for permission to use the photographs of Damascus photographer Fareed al-Kaylani; Marc Albert, for translating the French newspaper article; Joseph, Samira, Alain, and Habib Karout, for translating the Arabic newspaper article; Nagat Elesseily, for advice on everyday Arabic usage; David Sweet, copyeditor; and Desne Ahlers, proofreader. The translation of Asilah's journal was done by A&T Translators, Vancouver; errors in transcription are my own.

A very big thanks to the astute Annie Barrows, for her clear and enlightened editing; Sarah Malarkey, for believing in the project; and Jodi Davis, for managing the ebb and flow of constantly evolving material.

And a special thank-you to David Gay, for his unflagging support and, especially, for his well-trained eyes.

The photographs on pages 135 (bottom left) and 166 are of Bait Stambuli by Félix Bonfils, c. 1870. The sketch on page 132 (top) was redrawn from a painting by John Frederick Lewis, "In the Bezestein, El Khan Khalil, (Cairo) The Carpet Seller," 1860. The endpaper art is by W. H. Bartlett, from John Carne's *Syria, The Holy Land (etc.)*, London: Fisher, 1836.